Tame My Heart

MADDIE JAMES

SAND DUNE BOOKS

Tame My Heart

Maddie James

A Sweet Hart Inn Romance
Book 4

Copyright © 2018 Maddie James

Author: James, Maddie

Title: Tame My Heart

Description: 2nd Edition, Sand Dune Books

Subjects: Fiction / Romance / Contemporary | Small Town

Previously published under the title *Hot Crossed Buns*. *Tame My Heart* is a revised and updated edition, 2018.

Creative Work & Design by Jacobs Ink, LLC.

About Sweet Hart Inn

Welcome to Sweet Hart Inn... Where the kitchen is always warm and love is always on the menu.

Nestled on the peaceful edge of Falls Lake in the heart of the Blue Ridge Mountains, Sweet Hart Inn is more than a cozy bed and breakfast—it's a place where hearts heal, friendships form, and romance is served with a side of sass.

At the center of it all is Suzie Hart, a chef-turned-innkeeper whose recipes have a way of bringing people together (and finding their way into her books) —and sometimes, sparking unexpected love. Along with her (soon-to-be, maybe?) husband Brad, Suzie welcomes a delightful cast of characters through the inn's front doors, such as runaway brides, brooding bachelors, holiday guests, disgruntled daters, and more.

Whether you're looking for a heartwarming holiday escape, a second-chance romance, or a cozy story filled with culinary charm, the Sweet Hart Inn series delivers all the feel-good vibes you crave.

Bon Appetit! And enjoy.

Tame My Heart

Sweet Hart Inn, Book 4

What's a small-town cop to do when the love of his life bolts the second he pops the question? Call in the local matchmaker for backup, of course.

Katie Long has big dreams and no intention of being tied down—especially not by marriage. Her relationship with Harbor Falls police officer Chris Marks is perfectly fine as it is. Why does he insist on changing everything?

When Chris proposes, Katie panics. Heartbroken but determined, Chris turns to Suzie Hart, the town's resident chef and occasional cupid, to help set the perfect stage for romance. With candlelight, comfort food, and a sprinkle of matchmaking magic, Suzie gives Chris one last chance to prove he's the man who can tame Katie's restless heart.

But will Katie finally say yes...or run again before love can catch her?

Tame My Heart is spicy romance novella guaranteed to heat up your kitchen! Perfect for readers who love romance stories with:

- A commitment-shy heroine,
- A matchmaking innkeeper,
- A befuddled law enforcement hero,
- Foodie dating scenarios,
- Runaway bride vibes.

Prologue

Suzie Hart Matthews silently observed the contrast in the two scenarios presenting themselves in front of the Harbor Falls Methodist Church.

A smug and satisfied feeling passed over her as Nash Rhodes, tall, handsome, and wearing tight wranglers, ostrich boots, and a tauntingly sexy, black Resistol cowboy hat, strode down the concrete walk leading from the church while carrying his smiling and radiant Mary Lou Picketts, dragging the train of her wedding dress behind them.

A wedding dress she didn't get married in because she'd called off her wedding. Not to Nash, but to Barry Phillips. Thank God, the girl had seen the light in time.

Anyway, Suzie couldn't help but smile knowing she'd done good work. A matchmaker she was becoming, and a good one at that. Yes. Perfect. She had *perfectly matched* two more hearts and was quite proud of that fact, if she did say so herself.

As Nash disappeared with his bride into a late model pickup truck, her gaze swung to the other scenario.

She knew the young man standing on the porch steps of

the cottage across the street. He'd not lived in Harbor Falls long but she'd seen him around town. The woman he was talking, um, arguing with, was familiar enough. Suzie had known Katie Long since they were kids. The couple was making enough of a ruckus, however, for half of Harbor Falls to get to know them both darned quick.

Katie seemed mad as heck about *something*. Suzie watched her stride quickly toward a small red sports car parked in the drive while giving the man a piece of her mind with every step. He followed, arguing back and flailing his arms. Suzie found it difficult to hear the actual conversation over the engine of the pickup truck.

Nash and Mary pulled away from the curb and Suzie ambled toward her own car, trying not to eavesdrop.

Much.

What she did hear, however, sounded like a whole lot of trouble for the young man across the street. Chris Marks. One of Harbor Falls' finest young new police officers.

Katie got in the car and drove away. Fast. Suzie lingered only a moment and watched as Chris stood in the driveway looking after her, then finally hung his head and shuffled toward the house.

Chapter One

Katie Long's fingers trembled even though she had a death-grip on the steering wheel. White knuckles popped through the flush of her skin. Her heart was about to beat out of her chest and an icky, nauseous feeling was creeping into her stomach. Dammit. She felt flushed and clammy all at the same time, heat shooting from her cheeks all the way down to the tips of her fingers and toes. Cold chills simultaneously rippled across her back. She was madder than hell.

Get it under control, Katie!

Her sight blurred and she shook her head in an attempt to clear the glaze from her eyes. Not happening. With a quick gasp, she gunned the engine of her Mustang GT and whipped to a pull-off on the side of the road, gravel arcing behind her as she narrowly avoided a culvert.

"Damn backcountry mountain road," she sputtered.

She pressed the brake—much too hard, her body jolted forward with the rapid stopping of the vehicle—simultaneously avoiding bumping into the rock wall of the overlook. Letting out a ragged sob, she whacked her forehead on the steering wheel. She was tempted to bang her stupid brain against it.

Repeatedly.

Just in case repentance did come with beating one's head up against something hard, she gave her forehead a good hit at the thing.

"Ow. Dammit." She leaned in and rested her forehead against the cool steering wheel and for a moment, just breathed. In. Out. In. Out. The even breathing seemed to settle her stomach a little. Good. Last thing she wanted to do right now was puke.

At least she'd gotten out of Harbor Falls before she totally lost it. Wouldn't do to have anyone see her cry. To have *him* see her cry.

The sonofabitch.

Then the tears rolled. Her hands shook, her heart jumped out of her chest, and her brain spun. My God, was she experiencing a slow, tortuous unraveling? Then what the hell, she let loose with a steady stream of sobs. Tears spilled. So unlike her.

She was Katie Long!

She didn't cry.

She was tough.

Wild.

Crazy.

Left the boys and made *them* cry.

Lifting her head, she leaned back against the headrest and at last switched off the engine. Her gaze drifted over the lazy, hazy backdrop of the Blue Ridge Mountains spanning the horizon before her. Dusk was in the process of settling in the mountains with sunset happening behind her. A purplish glow of light and shadows danced in the hollows and valleys of the landscape before her.

No doubt the mountains were beautiful any time of day, and right now was no exception, but she could barely see the beauty beyond the fear in her heart that was slowly coloring everything off hue.

She swallowed, exhaled, and tried hard to let the scenery capture her. After a few moments, her breathing slowed again, and her chest stopped hurting so much. She gulped back a couple of errant sobs and swiped at her runny nose. Then closing her gritty eyes in an attempt to slow the circling images and thoughts running through her head, she tried to concentrate, to think through what had just happened.

Chris had turned the tables on her, that's what had happened.

She'd thought they were out for a night of dirty movies, monkey sex, and pizza. Instead, Chris had gone and done something stupid. Why did he have to ruin a perfectly good Saturday night? Dirty movies and sex had been their ritual for months. Their relationship had been fun, erotic, and flirty—and sometimes a little risky and kinky—but they both loved every minute of it. Katie was thrilled with the *no-talk-of-permanency* agreement and attitude of the *younger-than-her* police officer who enjoyed pleasing her sexually, in all the right ways and hitting every one of her buttons.

Why the shit had he gone all goody-two-shoes on her?

So unexpected.

Letting go of another long breath, she blinked and stared again over the dim horizon. What was she going to do now?

God, she must look a mess. She grasped the rearview mirror and angled it toward her, catching a ray of leftover sunlight. "Oh, good Lord in Heaven." Her face was splotched, shiny, and smudged in all the wrong places. Was that snot stringing back toward her ear? Gross.

"Damn you, Chris Marks," she whispered while rummaging for a napkin or a used tissue or *something* in the glove box to wipe the mucous out of her hair. "This is entirely your fault. We could be experiencing orgasmic pleasure at this very moment, and you had to go and ruin it all."

She found a tissue and dabbed at her eyes. "That'll teach you to ask me to marry you." Then she looked back into the mirror again and shook her head in disbelief and confusion.

He *had* asked her to marry him.

Got down on one knee.

Even had a ring.

Damn him!

Had he forgotten that she didn't want to settle down? That she didn't want the picket fence and two-point-five kids and the dog and mini-van? Hadn't she made that quite clear? Didn't he remember that she had plans for her life that may, or may not even, include him?

No. He didn't know about the plans because she'd never told him about her plans. Or her dreams and goals for the future.

Because those were *her* plans. Personal. And she didn't want him to know.

She just wanted a monkey sex and dirty movies kind of relationship. She wasn't the happily-ever-after type and that had been fine with him for months—but suddenly, obviously, *he was* the happily-ever-type? What the hell?

"Damn you, Chris," she sputtered again while dabbing at her face, "for going above and beyond the call of duty and doing the right thing." She sniffed and stared at the reflection of her eyes. "Thank you, but no thank you."

CHRIS MARKS STOOD at the edge of his driveway and watched the taillights of Katie's red Mustang fade out of sight. Shit. He'd screwed that up. What was he going to do now?

He knew she was having a hard time with things lately.

Ever since they got the news—the shocking and scary news that neither of them wanted to talk about or face—she'd been skittish and standoffish. But he truly thought his solution to their problem was the best one for both of them.

He'd expected her to take one look at him, breathe a sigh of relief, and melt into his arms. He wanted her to realize that all he wanted was to fix the problem and take care of her. To love her.

That's all he really wanted for the rest of his life. To love her.

Somehow, he'd gone and screwed it all up. *Dammit!*

Dragging his gaze from the fading rear-end of her car he stared at the scene across the street. Suddenly he was gut punched. A tall man with a cowboy hat carried a woman in a white wedding dress down the sidewalk of the church toward an idling pickup truck. They were kissing with each stride he took, her arms wrapped tightly around his neck. Watching them, his heart pounded. The cowboy put his smiling bride into the passenger side of the truck. Chris watched her scoot to the middle and the cowboy got in beside her. The driver revved the engine and they were off. A piece of the bridal veil caught in the door fluttered as they drove by.

Should be me. Should be us. How was he going to fix this?

Turning, he headed back to his house, deep in thought. Mentally, he ticked off his options. He could give her space. He could text her. He could call. He could send roses. He could apologize.

Climbing the steps, he halted and suddenly his chest felt tight. Why the hell should he apologize? All he did was tell her he loved her and ask her to marry him. What was wrong with that? Why should he apologize?

No. Never apologizing for that. He loved her and wanted her. Forever. Not ever apologizing for wanting what he wanted.

His hand resting on his front doorknob, Chris paused.

Go after her.

He pondered that. He didn't want to make things worse. He hoped they could work this out. It wasn't like it was their first argument. They'd had a couple of zingers the past few months. But this?

Her reaction had not only stunned but also wounded him to his core. He had never expected she would say no.

Go after her.

But he knew her. She likely wouldn't care much about him running after her and trying to talk sense into her. She would see that as condescending and patronizing. She'd probably be insulted. Yes, she had made it clear she didn't want commitment, and he'd been happy with sex and her company. Now things were different, given the circumstances.

Besides, he loved her.

He'd changed his tune.

She hadn't.

Probably, she would get madder and run faster and longer if he followed her. Should he risk that? He might never get her back then but if he didn't do *something*, would she think he had given up?

No. He would never give up.

But would she *think* that?

Go after her.

Dammit. Should he? His gut and his heart kept nagging—but his brain, his head, was getting in the way. Sensibly, he should give her space and let her cool off. Yet again, if he let her cool off too long, she'd start thinking and making other plans and before he would know it she'd find a solution herself and...

No. He had to go after her.

But where did she go? Home? The library? To one of her friends? Somewhere else?

Turning on his heel, he shoved a hand into his front jeans

pocket and found his keys. Didn't matter where, he would find her. Harbor Falls wasn't that big and—

He stopped and settled his thoughts for a moment, staring at the church across the street. He would have that moment one day, carrying Katie Long out of the church with her kissing him all the way. Yes.

And he would go to the ends of the earth to find her and make it happen if he had to. He had to make this right. He had to convince Katie that getting married was not a bad thing, no matter the crazy idea she had in her head.

His gaze drifted to a woman across the road standing by a car. Suzie Hart? He didn't know her well but saw her often at the bakery in the mornings. Seemed she was watching him.

Then she shouted. "Go after her!"

Chris nodded, threw up a hand, and headed for his pickup truck.

KATIE SAT in the car overlooking the mountains until it was dark. She didn't turn on her lights, just sat there in the chilly, February darkness and ruminated over the situation.

While she attempted to clear her head, the opposite was actually happening. Confusion spun inside her brain and her heart, only making her feel more conflicted and uneasy. Her thoughts jumped to Chris and how he must be feeling right now—which scared her more than anything did. Generally, she didn't care about how the guys felt when she left them. The fact that she was concerned about him was one of her greatest sources of confusion—and just proved that she really did love him, although she'd known that for weeks now.

Still, she'd made it quite clear from the beginning of their relationship how things would go with them. She didn't screw around when she was with a guy and they were in a couple relationship but she had told him quite specifically that he was not to expect a commitment—like, a long-term commitment. In other words, marriage. She would not tie herself down with that kind of obligation. She was responsible only for herself.

They could be a couple. They could have never-ending sex and plenty of it but there would be no ring or marriage certificate. Ever.

He'd agreed. He was fine with it.

Now, he'd pulled a switch. The *bastard*.

Oh, she knew why, and it was commendable of him but—

Lights flashed behind her as a vehicle rounded a curve then slowed. It crawled to a near stop and paused, headlight beams bouncing into her rearview mirror. She locked the car doors and prayed whoever it was would move on. Sitting quietly, she watched in the mirror as the vehicle backed up a little and turned into the pull-off, lights arcing behind her and flashing briefly into the car before the vehicle pulled up beside her.

It was too dark to make out much about it, or who was inside.

She waited, holding her breath, fingers poised on her ignition keys, not wanting any trouble from anyone who might be out for trouble tonight. Then her breath whooshed from her lungs when the vehicle door swung open, the light in the truck cab flashed on, and she could see Chris sitting there looking at her. He got out—one long leg at a time—left the door open, and leaned to look inside her passenger window. He knocked with a knuckle on the glass and jiggled her door handle.

Good Lord. He'd followed her.

"Katie? What are you doing up here? Let me in, honey. Let's talk." His face was backlit by the light from the cab.

"No! Go away Chris. Not now."

"Please? You don't need to be sitting out here all alone."

She laughed. "That's exactly what I need right now, Chris. I need to be alone with my thoughts. We can talk tomorrow."

"And tomorrow you will put me off again."

He was probably right. "No, I won't. Go away for now. Okay?"

"Let me just explain, darlin'."

She didn't respond. He could explain all he wanted but it wouldn't make a difference. She had to work through this by herself. He was getting antsy on the other side of the door, however, she could tell. He rose, paced back and forth toward his truck, and lowered again to look into the window.

"C'mon, Katie. It's chilly out here."

"You can sit in your truck."

"Helluva way to try to talk."

"I told you I don't want to talk."

He paused for a moment and she waited through the silence.

"Then what the hell do you want to do?" he blurted out.

Katie stared ahead. She knew exactly what she wanted. No thought. No confusion. She wanted him. Right here. Right now. Just down and dirty screwing her brains out. She lifted the handle latch, got out of the car and slammed the door, rounded the rear and faced him square on. "I want sex. Here. Right now. Take me, Chris."

She lifted her skirt and leaned into the side of the car. The metal was cold and her ass was bare and it was dark as sin on that side of this mountain but to hell with it. She wanted what she wanted.

"Now, Chris," she repeated. "Come and get me."

He reached for his belt.

Chapter Two

Chris sat hunched over his coffee cup, letting the steamy aroma drift to his nostrils. He inhaled long and deep, taking in the dark roast blend he started every morning with at Sugar High on Main. The ripples in the hot beverage swirled as he stirred in another spoon of sugar.

It was his second cup and he needed the high-octane java jolt this morning, complete with extra sugar. Having barely slept for several nights now, he knew he would need all the help he could get today to stay alert and coherent.

Lifting the cup to his lips, he slammed back the remainder and set the over-sized mug on the table with a clatter.

"Refill?"

"Yup."

He glanced up at Sydney Hart with a grimace. She smiled wide and filled him right back up.

"Long night?" she teased.

"Might say." He hunched over again and pulled his mug and the sugar bowl toward him.

Sydney snickered. "Hm. Sorry you were *up* all night, Chris."

He ignored the emphasis on the word *up*. She sat the carafe on the table and glanced out over the street in front of the shop. "Next time tell Katie you need your sleep. Otherwise, you are grumpy as hell in the morning. After all, Harbor Falls wants you alert and steady on your feet, Officer Marks. You know, with all this protecting we need around here." She laughed.

"*Hmpht*." Harbor Falls was about as crime-free as Mayberry. He grimaced into the mug.

"My, my," she drawled, "trouble in River City?"

"That's none of your beeswax." He sipped at the hot liquid.

Sydney rambled on. "Hm. Well now, isn't that Miss Katie over there as we speak? Heading toward the library?"

Chris dropped his spoon on the table, sloshing a bit of coffee over the side of the cup, and jerked his head up toward the direction Sydney was looking.

"Shit."

Picking up the coffee carafe, the bakery owner giggled and backed away, nodding at Chris' fellow officer, Matt Branson, heading toward the table. "Your coffee and Danish comin' right up, Matt."

Chris sank a little lower in his seat as Matt slid into the booth. "Gotta love living in a small town," he said, shrugging out of his jacket. "Not only does everyone know your name but what you want for breakfast, too."

"*Hmpht*," Chris uttered, still staring out the window, "and your business, too."

"Sounds like a personal problem."

You got that right. Personal as hell.

He heard the snap of a newspaper and figured Matt was reading the news, just like always. It was so stereotypical one almost had to laugh. Two of Harbor Falls' finest from the local police force meeting for coffee and doughnuts while the whole of Harbor Falls drifted by outside the coffee shop window. Here they were, Barney and Andy, waiting for a reason to race to the cruiser out front, on the off chance they would get to use their one bullet.

Matt had been on the force several years. Chris was a relative newcomer to Harbor Falls. He'd craved small-town living all his life, having grown up in Chicago suburbia. While on a vacation with an old girlfriend in the mountains, he'd discovered the charm of the town called Harbor Falls and all that came with it. The girlfriend didn't understand and they broke up not long after he told her he landed himself a job and was moving south. He'd been here two years and loved every minute of it. She went on with her life.

Funny, that breakup stung but he got over it quickly. This recent rejection from Katie had left him more than stung and he wasn't dealing with it very well. At. All.

That morning, however, his mind wasn't on his old girlfriend or on police business. He wasn't thinking about being cop-like. His thoughts roamed more toward other avenues. Like how to get Katie back into his bed. Back in his life. It had been nearly a week since they'd rendezvoused on the mountain. She'd been putting him off ever since and it was about to drive him crazy—in more ways than one.

Katie.

His Katie. Dammit.

His gaze transfixed on the scene across the street, he stared at her. He watched every slow and tortuous movement she made as she exited her car, reached for the rear side door, and bent to retrieve something out of the back seat. Slim-hipped, she wore a red, knee-length, ass-hugging skirt, tight enough to cup under her nicely rounded rear-end. His heartbeat picked up its cadence thinking about that round ass. Under him. On top of him. His hands gripping and squeezing. Not to mention her equally full and ample breasts heavy on his chest;

her waist-length brunette hair cascading over him while she rode him like a barrel-racing cowgirl....

Shit. He wiped his brow.

He couldn't drag his gaze away. Her backside swaying for the world to see—or for him to see?—she tugged her purse and a box out of the back seat of her shiny red Mustang GT.

The vixen.

She knew he sat there every morning getting his breakfast and drinking coffee with Matt. And she knew damned well how he liked to watch her. He'd whispered naughty words into her ear while they were intimate way too many times, talking about how hard he got watching her walk from the parking lot to the library, and how each and every time all he thought about was getting her into bed and....

He shook that thought off. Why in hell, after the argument they'd had the other night, and the quick and dirty fuck they'd had on the side of the road—only to end with an argument that sent them both hightailing it back home—was she sashaying that tempting ass of hers in front of him like that now? Today?

"Damn woman," he muttered, bringing the mug back to his lips. "Like a spoiled little girl who needs a spanking."

Matt slapped the newspaper down on the table.

Chris met his stare. "What?"

"All right. Spit it out. What's going on between you and Katie?"

Giving his head a slow shake, Chris drew up one corner of his mouth. "Not a damn thing."

"There's something."

"Nope. Nothing is going on between the two of us and that is the problem."

Matt leaned in. "She holding out?"

"Not speaking." He cleared his throat. "Yes, and holding out."

"Doesn't sound like Katie. What did you do?"

Chris mumbled. "Something stupid."

Sydney returned with Matt's Danish and black coffee and they silenced. She left as quickly. "Stupid?" Matt echoed.

"Yeah."

"Jesus, Chris. What the hell did you do?" He sipped his coffee.

Sidling his gaze back to Matt, he replied. "Asked her to marry me."

Matt spit coffee halfway across the table.

"Shit!" Chris jerked back. "You damned near spewed all over my uniform." He swiped at his pressed black shirt. "Costs me a buck-ninety-eight each to get my shirts cleaned and starched!"

Concentrating on wiping minute droplets of coffee off his badge, he avoided looking at Matt, who was staring a hole right through him. Heat radiated from his cheeks and he was embarrassed.

Yes, dammit, he had asked Katie to marry him. And she had flat out refused. Laughed and yelled at him. Pretty much told him it would be a cold day in hell...

"Why in God's name did you do that?"

His gaze rose. "I love her."

Matt cleared his throat. "Now Chris, don't get me wrong. You know I like Katie a whole helluva lot. But she's a wild filly, as wild as they come, and you think you're gonna tame her?"

He lowered his head and fiddled with his napkin. "Was trying."

"And how did you propose to do that? Katie made no bones about it when you started dating that she wanted to remain footloose and fancy free. I told you—and I won't say that *I told you so*—that you were getting into deep water. She's pretty new back in town, you know—well, she grew up here of course but she's just come back after years of living in the city—and you know she's been around the block a time or two. Hell, even when she was a teenager here at Harbor Falls High she had earned that love 'em and leave 'em reputation. Katie Long can't be tamed. Better men than you have tried. Her legacy in this town with men didn't disappear the ten years she was gone. She's such a damn contradiction, librarian by day, temptress at night. That was my biggest fear, that you'd fall head over heels in love with her and she'd break your heart." He paused and looked to his partner. "Dammit, I saw this coming."

Narrowing his gaze, Chris looked out the window. "For a man who said he wouldn't say, 'I told you so', you just did a damn good job of it."

Matt exhaled. They sat in silence for a moment. Looking back toward the library, Chris realized Katie was gone now. Shit. He'd missed her sway into the building. "I can tame her."

"Hm."

"No, really. I can."

Matt chuckled. "You're not going to give up, are you?"

"Nope."

"So how do you propose to tame her?"

"Sex."

"I thought you said she was holding out. How's that working for you?"

Chris grinned and eyeballed Matt. "With the palm of my hand."

"Excuse me?"

"She likes to be spanked."

Silence.

Chris angled his gaze toward Matt, whose left eyebrow now sported a significant arch.

"You don't say," his partner said. "Wow."

"I do say. Now, nothing real bad kinky and I would never hurt her—I don't want to dominate her at all, not really into that lifestyle shit—but she seems to respond to a little hanky-spanky action in the bun area."

Matt rubbed his chin. "I never would have thought."

Grinning, Chris added, "and right about now, I'd like to lay my hand flat across those—"

"Hot cross buns?"

Startled at the female voice coming from his right, Chris looked first to Matt, and then to the woman standing beside them. Suzie Hart-Matthews, Sydney's cousin and Matt's sister-in-law, stood staring at both men while holding out a tray of some kind of rolls with a crisscross of icing over the top.

"What?"

"Want to try my hot cross buns? It's a new recipe and Sydney is going to give them a go here at *Sugar High*. I thought you might want a sample. Fresh out of the oven. And hot."

Chris was definitely thinking about hot buns, and about crossing them with the palm of his hand, but what Suzie offered up at the moment wasn't going to fit the bill.

He rose. "No thanks, ma'am. Maybe another time. I've got some business to tend to."

He tipped his head, glanced at Matt, tossed a couple of bills on the table, and left.

THINGS WERE SLOW THIS MORNING. Thank goodness.

Katie stood behind the checkout desk, glanced over the near-empty library, and decided that Saturday mornings lately were nothing like they used to be. Oh, they had the regular traffic and busy times, but nothing like she wanted. When she was younger and growing up in Harbor Falls, moms and kids would come to the library for story hour on Saturdays. She had always enjoyed that time when she'd worked there shelving books during her high school years.

But story hour was canceled a few weeks ago when the library board realized they were competing with Saturday morning soccer and cheerleading. Story hour now happened on Tuesday and Thursday mornings, targeted only for preschoolers and stay-at-home moms. Around here, most moms worked, so the crowd was dwindling and she worried story hour would be gone all together one day.

Also used to be that the old-timers came in to read the newspaper or catch up on gossip on Saturday morning. Now they head to *Sugar High* across the street for coffee and Facebook.

Interesting sign of the times.

It troubled her, this occasional lack of library business. She loved books. They were her life. A self-proclaimed bookaholic, she devoured most any book she could get her hands on. Not to mention, she was writing one herself. Had been since she graduated from college five years ago. No one knew that, of course. She kept the one thing to herself. That and her other dream. Oh, everyone in Harbor Falls thought she was perfectly happy coming back home after all these years—she'd worked in Charlotte after college—and taking over the librarian position. Especially since the job had stayed vacant for almost two years. And yes, she was very glad to get the job and start building back the library's offerings, but this recent slump had her a little unnerved.

She needed her job—at least for a while longer, until she got a handle on the next phase of her life. Her dream. Her goal.

You see, she wanted more.

Usually, she anticipated and appreciated the hustle and bustle of Saturday mornings, the rushing off into the stacks to help someone find a book, the rustling of newspapers and magazines in the reading corner, the hum of the old copier, and low mumblings and occasional giggles of children. But today, truth be known, she was glad for the silence. Her brain cluttered with recent events, she welcomed the quiet. Besides, there was plenty of work to do today. Bea Brammel, her library assistant, had been off work all week with sick kids and as a result, there were dozens of books to be shelved from the week. She wasn't sure yet if Bea was coming in today. Katie hadn't checked the library phone messages yet.

She would check there after she shelved for a while. "No time like the present," she said aloud, drifting toward a cart full of disorganized books. She pushed it toward the stacks then stopped at the end, working through the volumes to organize them a bit before heading into the stacks. She looked forward to spending time handling and categorizing this morning. The menial work would keep her mind from spinning.

Still, as she idly shelved book after book, her thoughts subconsciously turned to the one thing she didn't want to think about.

Chris. Damn him.

She knew, of course, that he was surprised as hell at her reaction a few nights ago. In the four months they had dated, everything had gone so well. In fact, it was the one relationship she'd had thus far that felt promising. Almost. That almost part, however, was more to do with her than him.

She cared for Chris a whole helluva lot. Might even be falling in love with him. Hell, she probably *was* in love with him. They'd had good times together and the sex was, well, exceptional and explosive. Most of all—and this was the thing that frightened her more than anything—they could talk.

So much so, in fact, that she had damned near shared her hopes and dreams with him not long ago. She'd never done that with any man. Never.

That scared her.

Tremendously.

He was getting too close and she was letting him in. Surprisingly, she had almost convinced herself that it was okay. That being part of a couple with Chris was a good thing. Then... Then, dammit, things went haywire and instead of logically talking and working things out, he popped the stupid question on her. Why couldn't he have waited a little longer, until she was good and convinced that this couple thing could even, possibly, be permanent?

That was all she had needed. A little time.

Her brain started spinning, rerunning the old scripts in her head. Love 'em, leave 'em. Don't get attached. She didn't do permanent. Hadn't she made it clear that she didn't do forever? That she wasn't interested in anything more than dating and having fun and living in the moment?

Crap.

Most men were fine with her Devil-may-care attitude about relationships. She counted on that. They weren't looking for deep commitment. That was her safety net. She wasn't looking for commitment, either, because commitment would get in the way of her hopes and dreams.

Chris, unfortunately, was now looking for commitment. Even if he'd never verbalized it. He'd moved to this Podunk town *by choice*, hadn't he? She'd moved back to Harbor Falls because it was a stepping stone. A good job that paid well and allowed her to save money. Living in her grandmother's house rent-free was also a bonus. Her goal was to put back enough funds to live on for a full year so she could finish writing her book, and get it spit-shined and polished and off to an agent. Then after the book sold—of course it would because if anyone knew books, she did—she was going to find a nice quiet beach house somewhere and live out the rest of her life, writing her own stories rather than shelving those of others.

She was giving herself a year to devote to the book and she had to make her dream happen in that year. That was her plan. Then this sexy police officer popped into the library one day, two months after she'd gotten the job, and her plans went south.

What the hell happened to her life? Her plans?

Chris Marks happened. That's what.

AFTER SITTING in his cruiser for the past hour, Chris was glad to get out and stretch his legs. As he strolled across the street, he glanced up to the clock on the town hall building and noted the time. Two minutes before noon. The old clock was a minute slow, everyone in town knew that, so he had only a minute to spare.

He glanced to the library door.

There she was. Bea. Leaving. She was always the first one out the door. Katie was usually an hour or so behind.

He picked up his stride. The library closed at noon.

Just as Bea turned to lock the door, he sidled up beside her, grasped her arm, and put a finger to his lips as she turned to look at him.

"Shh..." he sounded and slipped inside. She smiled and locked the door behind him.

Good ol' Bea.

Inside, the library was still and quiet. He stopped for a moment to let his eyes adjust to the lower light in the building. A shuffling sound came from the rear.

Ah, yes. There you are my sweet little vixen.

Creeping through the empty library, he glanced back through each aisle of books until he came upon the last one, closest to the wall. He hesitated a second, then peeked around the corner.

There.

Halfway into the stack, he caught sight of long silky legs and a red skirt hitched up over her right hip, and grinned. Katie stood partway up the ladder, at least four rungs up, braced against the bookshelf. Her sinful derrière at his eye level, one foot rested on a shelf while she leaned to place a book precisely in its Dewey Decimal System home.

In three silent strides, he was behind her, each fist gripping the ladder on either side of her hips. His foot was on the first rung of the ladder before she had a clue he was anywhere near.

Chapter Three

Katie felt the tingles race up the back of her calves about the same time she realized Chris was behind her. It wasn't the first time he'd slipped into the library and they'd had mad, crazy sex in the stacks. Still angry and confused, but turned on at the same time, she wasn't sure which emotion to push away. Not today. Sex wasn't happening today. In the stacks, or between her sheets. She had to resist.

He took another step up the ladder and his left hand moved to her thigh, inching up inside her skirt.

"No pantyhose, good girl."

"You know I hate pantyhose."

"What about panties?" One hand smoothed over her bare hip under her skirt.

"You know I don't do panties. You shouldn't be here," she whispered.

"That never stopped you before," he replied.

"I'm really mad at you."

He rose higher and pressed her against the ladder. His breath was hot on her neck. "That never stopped you before," he repeated, nibbling behind her ear.

He was right. Dammit.

And he was hard. His hand snaked up to her waist, raising her skirt. The hot length of him scorched her bare backside.

His lips branded the side of her neck. "Umhm. Shit, you are hot."

"Hot and mad."

"Forget about that."

Forget about it? How could she do that? Her brain always went to mush when he was around. "Are you are insane?"

"No, just crazy for you. C'mon, Katie. Let's talk about what happened. You won't answer my calls."

"For a very good reason."

"I want to be inside you."

Her breathing quickened. "No."

"Katie...."

Sandwiched between his body and the ladder, she felt precariously perched. Like between a rock and a hard place. The rock being the fact that she was mad as hell at him, and the hard place being, well, his hard place.

Which she wanted like there was no tomorrow. But no.

"Sex the other night didn't solve anything Chris. Did it? It's not going to solve anything today, either."

He chuckled and nuzzled her neck from behind. "It will solve both of us getting releasing a bit of pent-up tension."

"And a few weeks ago that would have been fine but not now. Get down, Chris. If you want to talk, we will talk. But not like this."

He chuckled. She thought she heard the quick whiz of his zipper. Twisting back as much as she could, she looked him square in the eyes and said, "No. I mean it."

She wanted him. She really did. And riskily balanced there on the library ladder was exactly the kind of excitement she liked, no craved, when it came sex. She liked to be daring and bold and risky. But not today. The ladder squeaked and rocked beneath them and she trembled with the instability of their stance and the potential danger of the situation. It only made her want him more. She craved an orgasm.

She'd be working overtime with her vibrator tonight.

The shelf creaked.

Chris rocked methodically against her backside.

She exhaled, reached back, dug her fingers into his thigh, and squeezed. "Damn you," she hissed.

"You love it," he groaned.

"You wish."

Chris pinned her tighter to the ladder. The thing shifted and scooted to the right.

"Gonna fall," she breathed.

"I have you." He drew her closer into his embrace. "I'll keep you safe. Won't let you fall, babe."

Without warning, tears pricked behind her eyelids. Safe. Yes. Since the beginning of their relationship, he had made her feel safe. "If you fall we both fall," she said quietly, then wondered about the subtle undertones to the words she had just said.

Chris whispered against the back of her neck, "Honey, I've already fallen. You know that. I just need for you to fall with me."

Again, she pushed out a breath and tried to steady herself. "Chris, please," she whispered.

He hesitated, sighed, and then moved. "All right, Katie. I'm backing down now," he told her. "Stay still until I'm on the floor. Don't worry. I'm right behind you."

He smoothed his hands over her backside, adjusting her skirt as he descended. Katie missed having him so close. His warmth left her back and suddenly, she didn't like that feeling. It was somewhat nice, him having her back.

"C'mon down, Katie," he said softly. "I'm right here."

Yes. And that was the problem. He was there and he

wasn't going away, was he? And she'd fallen into the trap of his potent sexual appeal. Maybe his love.

She backed down the ladder and in one motion, Chris spun her around to face him and kissed her mouth. She didn't, couldn't, resist.

The kiss—delivered long, slow, and with a sensual urgency—left her lips tingling.

Breaking away, Chris pulled back, looking into her face. Katie let their gazes mingle while her heartstrings tangled with her brain. No one had ever looked at her, or kissed her, like he did. Always with such intensity. Love? It was confusing as hell. He brushed a stray lock of hair from her forehead and looked deeper into her eyes, unflinching. She saw longing and hope and a little bit of hurt in their reflection.

"Pick you up at eight?" he said softly. "We can talk. Then how about a movie and makeup sex later?" He waggled his brows.

Her insides battled her response. Before she could contemplate the right answer, she blurted out, "No, Chris..."

"Katie..."

She put him at arm's length, shaking her head. "No. No movie. No makeup sex. Please, Chris, give me some space. I need time to adjust to all of this."

He stepped back and stared, looking her up and down. "I don't want to argue with you, Katie."

She nodded. "I know. I don't want to argue either."

"So what are we going to do?"

She blew out a breath. "You are going to let this idea about getting married go for a while, and I'm going to process."

He shook his head. "Not happening."

"You have to Chris."

Still shaking his head, he said, "No. Because the moment I let it go, you will get other ideas. I am not giving up. I plan to be in your face until you agree to talk this through. If that's not this morning, or this evening, fine, but Katie Long, just know that I am here to stay. I am not going to let you forget that I love you and that I want to marry you. I'll leave now but make no mistake, I will bug you to the ends of hell and back if I have to until we come to some sort of resolution."

She stared back. "Even if it's not the one you want?"

Katie felt the intensity of his returned glare. "That's not going to happen."

CHRIS LEFT THE LIBRARY, exhaling long as the heavy wooden door came to an unsatisfying soft close behind him. Shoving his hands in his pockets, he glanced across the street to Sydney's place and thought about heading over just so he could sit in his usual spot, drink a pot of coffee, and stare at the library waiting for Katie to leave—then he realized how pitiful and stalker-like that sounded.

She wanted space. Time. Watching her like a hawk wasn't going to do that and it wasn't good for him either. He needed to retreat for a few hours.

It was Saturday afternoon and he was off duty for the rest of the day. As he headed for his patrol car in the parking lot, he contemplated how he could fill up the next several so he wouldn't dwell on Ms. Katie Long too much. He needed a distraction.

He could bug the guys down at the station but they would ask too many question he didn't want to answer. Maybe he could head over to the Youth Center and challenge some kids to a game of basketball. That might be a good way to burn off some pent-up steam and sounded like a good idea. Besides, he liked to connect with the kids when he could. Most of them needed a positive male role model and he occasionally filled that role with a few of them.

Decision made, he headed toward his car when some commotion and chatter across the street caught his ear. His gaze swung toward Rick's Café and he watched a pack of older women wander from the gift shop next door—a place called *Romantically Yours* that was owned by Sydney's sister, he'd recently learned—and into the bar and grill. Pausing, he studied the five ladies as they rattled on.

He'd seen them before while drinking his coffee and socializing at Sugar High. Most Saturday mornings they headed into the gift shop about ten o'clock in the morning, stayed there for a couple of hours, and then about noon they would head over to Rick's place.

This town and its people sure did have their quirks.

He'd not been in Harbor Falls long—two years, he'd learned from many of the residents, was not long enough to be called local yet—but he'd definitely gotten a feel for the makeup of the town and the close-knit relationships of the town folk. He knew that was something that would take him a while to achieve but he was determined he would.

"In about twenty years," Matt had told him once. Chris scoffed but knew he was likely to speak the truth.

Glancing at the town clock, Chris realized it was past lunchtime. Perhaps he'd head over to Rick's and get a bite himself before basketball but then nixed that idea as he crossed North Main Street and drifted toward the gift shop instead. Without much thought at all, he went inside.

A tall, pretty woman looked up from behind the counter as he crossed the threshold and stepped into the shop.

"Good afternoon," she said. "May I help you?"

It was Sydney's sister, he knew. She occasionally stopped in to Sugar High for a skinny mocha. Funny how one quickly learned townsfolks' morning beverages of choice. Chris glanced around the shop. Froo-froo met him from every angle as he blinked to let his eyes adjust to the low light and subtle ambiance.

"Hello," he said, stepping on inside. "I think I'm just looking. I'm Chris Marks."

The woman smiled. "Yes. I know. You're on the police force. I see you most mornings next door."

He smiled and chuckled. "I'm sure. I'm addicted to Sydney's pastries."

A half-grin crossed the woman's face. She put out her hand out as Chris approached the counter. "I'm Grace Hart Price. Sydney's sister."

Chris took her hand and shook it. "Wow, the Harts are everywhere." He laughed. "I'm friends with Matt Branson on the force. I guess his wife Shelley is your...?" He paused.

"Cousin," Grace said. "Shelley and Suzie are sisters. Sydney and I are sisters. Our mothers are sisters so we're cousins." She laughed then and finished fiddling with some tags on the counter. "The four of us had a grand old time growing up, I tell you. We gave our parents and grandparents a run for their money, that was for certain."

Nodding, Chris could understand that. "Four girls and I'd say you're all about the same age, right?"

"Yes. All four born within three years. We were a mighty little force of estrogen." She laughed again. "What can I do for you today, Chris?"

He glanced about the shop again, then back to Grace. "To be perfectly honest, I don't know. But I have a question."

"Sure. What can I help you with?"

He leaned into the counter. "I'm curious, really. Totally none of my business but what's up with the group of ladies that just left?" He ticked his head toward the door.

Grace leaned toward Chris too, resting her elbows on the glass countertop. "Oh, it's so secret," she whispered.

He cocked an eyebrow. "Oh?"

"Umhmm." Grace nodded, and then glanced about, putting her finger to her lips. "Sh. It's the weekly book club." Then she rose and laughed.

Chris chuckled too. "Book club, huh? Then lunch at Rick's Café?"

"Exactly. We like to keep business in the family. My husband owns the café next door, you know?"

Chris had experienced a few happy hours there with Katie. "Yes, great food, good company. Local crowd."

"He prides himself on all three."

Chris did know that Rick was her husband. Grace stepped around the counter and headed toward a table of stationary and paper items. He watched her smooth movements and decided she was aptly named. The tall, willowy woman, he'd heard, used to be a dancer. "Quirky bunch, aren't they?" he finally said.

"Oh yes. The stories..." Grace waved a hand and turned, her eyes big and round, a mannerism that southern women pull off so well. "Why, I could go on and on about those ladies but I'm sure you don't have time and... What were you looking for coming in here, Mr. Marks?"

He had no clue. "Like I said, I'm not sure. I hope you can help."

"Are you looking for a gift? A card? I have a variety of eclectic items and an assortment of useless trinkets." She rounded the counter and glanced about. "All in the name of love, of course."

She did indeed have a unique collection.

"I buy from all over the world," she added. "Some things are antique, some modern, some items just funky and quirky, or rather Bohemian. All totally romantic, I assure you. I ship anywhere for a price and will deliver locally."

That last part piqued his interest. "Deliver?"

She smiled. "Of course. My husband comes in handy that

way at times." She headed deeper into the store. "So, are you looking for a gift for a girlfriend? Potential girlfriend? An *I'm-sorry* gift, or a *let's-make-up* gift?"

He thought about that. "I think I could safely say that covering all of those bases would probably be a good thing."

She laughed and poked through some items on a shelf. "Do you have any idea how often I hear that?"

Chris could only imagine.

"Hm. Let's see," she continued. "Something sweet? Something sexy? Something serious. Something..." She paused, still looking, moving things around. "Or..." She turned back and grinned again, lifting a scrap of lacy fabric off the table and dangling it on her fingertip. "Something a little more wicked?" She winked.

Chris watched her turn and head toward a rack of skimpy lingerie.

"Something a little more wicked would be perfect," he told her. *I think.* How did he know any more with Katie? Then as an afterthought, he added, "Wicked but sophisticated at the same time. Is that possible?"

Smiling, she crooked her finger. "I have the perfect thing."

KATIE KNEW Chris wasn't kidding about being persistent but she hadn't expected this long of a drought without contact. It had been hours since she'd seen him earlier in the day and he'd not called. Not once. It was starting to get a little pathetic that she kept looking at her cell phone to see if he'd left a text or a voice mail.

Nope. She guessed he'd changed his mind and was leaving her alone.

And she'd asked for that, so why was she concerned?

No, she hadn't asked, she had demanded. It appeared he had listened.

But this radio silence was a little unsettling. The lack of communication hadn't given her time to think—in fact, her brain just kept rolling around the notion that he hadn't called.

What good was that?

No good. None at all.

Pathetic was right.

At seven o'clock that evening, she decided to take a shower and get into her nightgown. With no plans, and no prospects of anyone coming over, she just wanted to get comfortable and chill for a while. Finished with her shower about twenty minutes later, she returned to her living room and out of habit, glanced at her cell phone.

Groan. No calls. No texts.

She heaved a huge sigh that puffed out her cheeks.

Time. She needed time. She'd told him that and he was evidently going respect her wishes and listen to what she wanted. And while she missed him terribly, and felt a little unsettled not hearing from him, she needed this time to think. Plan. Figure out what the hell she was going to do.

If she could only concentrate on that. Distraction was eating up her thinking time.

What the hell am I going to do?

She glanced to the sofa and then the television. Watch a movie, that's what. *I am going to settle into my sofa with my quilt and a bowl of popcorn and my cat. And for a couple of hours, I'm going stick my head deep in the sand and pretend none of this is happening.*

Ostrich. She just wanted to be a freaking ostrich for a while. Tugging the quilt up around her, she reached for her remote control. Her cell rang and without thinking, she picked it up, glanced at the face and saw Chris's name, and hit the talk button.

She held her breath and didn't say a word.

"Katie?"

She remained silent, not sure what to say.

"Katie, honey, can we talk now? Look, we'll do this on your terms. I'll stop pushing. I'm willing to give you space and I'm trying real hard. You just have to tell me what those terms are. Okay?"

Sighing, she listened but didn't respond. After a moment, he started talking again.

"Can I come over and we just talk this through?"

Katie's chest was taut. She wanted to inhale and let out another huge breath but her lungs wouldn't cooperate. Her chest felt too tight. If she said yes to his question, they were in for a night of discussion, and then probably sex, and that wasn't what they needed right now. Besides, she didn't know if she was up for any of it. If she said no—and if she kept saying no—would he finally give up and go away?

Was that what she wanted? No. Not really.

"My terms?" she asked.

He quickly responded. "Yes, honey. You call the shots."

She would call the shots. That's what she wanted right? Or was it?

So confusing.

"I don't know. Let me think about it Chris." She heard him start to say something but his voice was gone as soon as she hit the end call button.

Immediately, her phone pinged with a text message. *I love you*, Chris had typed.

"I love you too," she whispered.

She turned off the sound on her phone and tossed it to the other end of the sofa. Plucking up a piece of popcorn, she drew the quilt around her and punched at the remote control to start the movie. Her cat, Molly Mae, carefully stepped across the cover and curled into her side. Katie scratched the back of her Calico head.

Then her doorbell rang. Shit. Was he outside on her porch? If so, she wasn't in the mood for this and felt her temper flare a little. She unwrapped herself from the blanket and untangled from the cat, crossed the room, grabbed the front door handle and jerked the thing open, and said loudly, "I told you—"

She stopped. It wasn't Chris standing on her porch.

A man stared and said, "Katie Long? I have a delivery."

"Oh?" The wind yanked out of her sails, she was quite discombobulated. "Yes. I'm Katie."

"Here you go. Enjoy." He smiled and handed her a fancy-wrapped box, complete with pretty red and pink bows and a card taped to the top. She took it. "Thank you."

The man tipped his head and turned, jogging down her porch steps. She watched him walk the length of her sidewalk and get into a car. Then finally, she looked at the gift in her hands and shut the door.

Inside, she moved back to the sofa and set the box on the ottoman. She drew the quilt back around her and stared at the box for several long minutes. Molly Mae crept back into her lap and she mindlessly stroked the cat's head. Obviously, the gift was from Chris. What had he gone and done now? Did she want to look tonight, or wait until tomorrow?

Pushing out a breath, she set the popcorn aside and reached for the box. Slowly, she peeled off the ribbons and tape, then before going any further, opened the card and read it.

I can't wait to see this on you. Love, Chris.

Sighing, she went back to her task. The lid gone now, she pushed back filmy pink tissue paper to reveal a pretty, red silky nightgown.

She lifted it out of the box, tears stinging her eyes. The

gown was low cut with spaghetti straps and very form fitting. Classy and sexy.

Like I'll be able to wear this in a month.

Without warning, she burst into tears. "Dammit!"

Katie jumped up. The quilt and box fell. Popcorn bounced on the hardwood floors. Molly Mae skittered off toward the bedroom. "I don't freakin' cry! What the hell is wrong with me?"

Collapsing again on the couch, she let out another sob. "Hormones. Stupid, stupid, baby hormones." Snatching up the quilt, she cocooned herself inside and lay in a fetal position on the sofa. It was a poor attempt at blocking out the world, she knew, and one that wouldn't work anyway because all her troubles were inside the darned thing.

Chapter Four

It was unusual for Chris to be sitting in his booth at Sydney's on a Sunday morning. Since he and Katie had been dating, he usually woke up in her bed, sampling some of her morning offerings. The fact that he was sitting in a cold vinyl booth at seven o'clock in the morning, drinking coffee that had seen a better brew, while staring a hole in the Formica tabletop before him, told him one thing.

He was a pitiful sucker.

A goner.

And it wasn't just about the sex. He loved Katie. He'd be damned if he would lose this battle. He would have her. And for the rest of his life.

"Sassy little spitfire."

Someone slid into the booth seat across from him. "What the hell are you doing here on a Sunday morning?"

Matt.

"Hell if I know." He sipped the bad brew again and jerked his head up. "Hey Sydney, you got any more coffee? I need something a little stronger. This is pretty darned weak this morning!" He raised his cup in the air. "And bring Matt one of those new buns or something. On me."

Matt put his hand on Chris's arm, and he lowered the cup. "Down boy. What's got you riled?"

"Need I remind you?"

Chuckling, Matt agreed. "Saw you in the window as I went by. Shelley sent me out for a Sunday paper."

"Too bad they don't deliver up on the mountain."

Matt shrugged. "Doesn't matter to me but Shelley likes to keep tabs on the world a bit.

So, what happened now?"

"Nothing."

"Still?"

"Yeah."

Silence.

Sydney sidled up to the table. "Here's a fresh pot, Chris. You sure are a sour puss this morning. Slide that cup over here." She gave Chris the eye, then glanced to Matt and sat an empty cup in front of him, filling both cups. "What's brought the two of you out on a Sunday morning?"

Chris harrumphed.

Matt rolled his eyes, looked up at Sydney, and ticked his head Chris's way. "He can tell you his story. I'm just out for the paper. Shelley sent me."

Sydney nodded. "Ah. That girl always did like to read the Sunday paper in bed."

"Which means that I'm up early to get it." He shrugged. "It's all right though. The girls are at her mom's and she deserves to sleep in occasionally. Besides, with the baby coming..."

Sydney set the coffee pot on the table with a bang. "What did you just say, Matt Branson?"

Chris looked at Matt, who suddenly had a deer-in-the-headlight look. Matt and Shelley were having a baby?

"Ah, shit, Sydney," Matt said. "Please don't go spreading that around. Shelley didn't want me to tell anyone yet and she was going to surprise the family next weekend at the reunion. Please act surprised."

Baby. Matt and Shelley were *having a baby.* Chris gulped a drink of hot coffee, grimaced, and then glanced away. He could hear Matt and Sydney chatting beside him but didn't hear a word they said. A baby. A thud landed deep in his gut.

This was a happy occasion. So much so that Shelley wanted to surprise her family. And here he was in the same position and couldn't even talk about it. Something not right with that picture....

"Chris?"

He turned when Sydney poked him. "What?"

"So what's up with you?"

He shook his head. "Nothing."

"All hell, Chris," Matt prodded. "Tell her. Maybe she can help."

Glancing at Sydney, he arched a brow. "I doubt it."

Leaning into the table, Sydney replied. "Don't underestimate me, Chris Marks. I've got skills."

He had to chuckle at that. "I'm sure you do, Syd, but this I gotta fix myself."

Rising, she exchanged a glance with Matt, who shrugged and said, "He's got woman troubles."

Chris pushed back from the table. "Hell, Matt!"

"Well, you do! Maybe Sydney has some pointers."

She interjected. "I knew something was going with you and Katie. I can tell these things."

Matt sat back with his coffee. "It runs in the family."

Chris had no clue what that meant. "I'm good. I don't need a woman to solve my woman problems." He stared at Matt. "As you so eloquently put it."

"Well, you need to do something other than sulk over your coffee every morning."

"You just need to get back on the horse," Sydney told him.

"What?"

"Go out on a date."

"She won't go."

Sydney rolled her eyes. "Not with Katie, you dufus, with another woman. I could find you someone easy-peasy. I mean, like women walk in here all of the time. Like... Oh look, there is Lyssa Larkin right now." She pointed out the window.

Chris followed her pointing finger to a woman who walked by the bakery about this time every morning, with about six dogs leading her down the sidewalk.

"Her?"

"Of course! She's single and she's pretty and she..."

"She's older than me."

Sydney shrugged. "Well, maybe. I'm not sure."

"She's always walking those dogs." He watched her for a moment. "Oh, there they go again."

"That's because she's a puppy nanny. You know, she boards and trains dogs and stuff. What?"

"The dogs. They got loose again." It happened a couple of times a week.

"Oh, hells bells."

Matt stood. The three of them, Sydney, Chris, and Matt watched while the tangle of dog flesh righted themselves and Lyssa recovered, stomping on leashes and snatching them up post haste.

"False alarm," Matt said.

"She's getting better at that," Chris added.

"Most days," Sydney chimed in. "Sure you don't want me to ask her for you, Chris?"

He shook his head. Chris couldn't see himself with the puppy nanny. "No, I don't think so."

"You could give it a try. It might make Katie wise up."

Or jealous. He didn't want Katie to be jealous. He had managed to soften her somewhat from madder-than-a-fire-cracker to soft-fluttering-flame, but she was still refusing to talk. He just wanted her to come around to his way of thinking. Shaking his head, he said, "No. I'm not going out on a date with another woman. That would send all the wrong messages."

Sydney sighed. "You're sure?"

"I'm positive."

The bell on the door tinkled and all three of them looked to see who was coming in. Sydney took a step away from the table. "Hi Mary Lou. Scone du jour today and the house brew?"

The woman nodded, glanced to the men, and said, "Yes, please, Sydney. Thank you!" She moved off to the opposite end of the bakery to a table in the corner. Chris watched her pull things out of her bag and set them on the table.

"Mary Lou is taken," Sydney said.

Chris looked up. "I'm not interested in her, Sydney."

"Well, you were looking."

"I was looking because she's there every day, same time, doing the same stuff, day in and day out. Her life must be boring." He'd also seen her at the library late in the day too, when he'd dropped by to see Katie. She and Katie chatted from time to time.

Sydney laughed. "Her life is what she made of it. Besides, she's working. She's her own boss so she can work anywhere and she chooses to work here often. Hey, isn't that what you do when you come in here? Work?" She laughed and swatted Chris on the shoulder.

He frowned. "That's not funny, Syd."

But she kept giggling, putting the back of her hand to her mouth. "Well, it was a little. But back to Mary Lou. She wasn't having much luck in the relationship department either until Suzie stepped in. Right Matt?"

"Oh yeah. Suzie doesn't give up."

Chris was confused. "I have no idea what you are talking about."

"We know," Sydney said. "It's a family thing. Anyway, Suzie matched Mary Lou up with Nash Rhodes when he was here a few weeks ago. Remember? So that's why she's taken. Mary Lou and Nash are getting married as soon as he gets off the road from his current tour. I hear they are building a cabin up in the mountains. That right, Matt?"

He nodded. "Sure enough. There was some acreage for sale between my place and the lodge. Nash snatched it up before he left on tour."

Sydney sighed. "I just love a happily ever after."

Chris felt like the two of them were talking in code. Then he realized they were both staring at him. Was Mary Lou the woman he saw at the church that day with the cowboy in the black hat? "What?"

Matt rose. "All right. Enough is enough." He glanced toward the counter. "Sydney?

Pop those pastries in a bag and give us a couple of coffees to go. We're going to the source." He grasped Chris' sleeve and pulled him to his feet. "C'mon. We're going to Suzie's."

"What? I can get coffee and pastries here. I'd rather sit and..."

"And mope yourself to death. Sit here and wait, hoping that Katie walks by. No, not happening. Besides, we're not after Suzie's coffee or buns. We're going for something else."

Chris stared at him. "What are you talking about?"

A sly grin broke Matt's face. "Don't you know? Besides being a cookbook author, my sister-in-law is a matchmaker. So far, she is two-for-two. Let's see what she can do with the miserable likes of you."

KATIE MADE it through the night. She slept only a few hours but that was okay. Her head a little clearer now than yesterday, she rose about four o'clock in the morning, stumbled to the kitchen to make coffee, and then mug in hand headed for her favorite chair in the sunroom.

She recalled sitting out there with her grandmother early in the mornings when she was a little girl and had spent the night. Grammy was always up early—perhaps not as early as Katie was up today. Having grown up on a farm, and "up with the chickens" every day, it was difficult for her to break the habit. When Katie stayed over, she liked getting up early too, because Grammy always had crisp sugar cookies with her coffee and she'd let Katie have some with her milk.

Besides, she and Grammy had talks and Katie learned so much. She missed her grandmother like crazy and wished she were here right now to discuss her recent *issue.*

Katie's mother wouldn't have approved of the cookies—and perhaps not the talks—because according to her, sugar cookies were definitely not proper breakfast food, and Katie's mom and grandmother didn't exactly get along. But Grammy would smile and wink and say, "What your mother doesn't know won't hurt her."

Leaning back in the easy chair, Katie put her feet up on the ottoman. She smiled, thinking of Grammy and her matter of fact, pull-no-punches ways. She'd been a flower child in the sixties and had grown up on free love and no responsibilities—until she met Katie's grandfather. That was a story Katie always loved to hear. Gramps died a good decade before Grammy and Katie knew she had missed him terribly.

She had grown up to be a lot like her in many ways. Probably Grammy's influence led her down the path of "what people don't know won't hurt them." She found it interesting that years later, she was living in Grammy's house, and smiled. Katie had definitely attached herself to her grandmother's philosophies over the years, especially with relationships.

And it hadn't hurt her. Had it?

Of course, Grammy changed a little when she met Gramps. Would Katie change because of Chris?

Katie had never been dishonest with anyone. She just kept to herself, didn't tell things that didn't need to be said, and often let people wonder. "Your business is yours, Katie Marie," Grammy would say, "The whole town doesn't need to know." Many people assumed she was distant and aloof because of it and in some ways, she was. Her private life was no one's business but hers—she was definitely not one of those millennials who lived on social media and plastered every action and thought into the cyber-sphere.

Grammy would have hated Facebook.

For as outgoing as she appeared on the outside, Katie was a secret introvert and book nerd on the inside. Today, she planned to play book nerd up all day long and forget her troubles for a while. She might even carry things over to Monday, since it was President's Day and the library was closed.

Setting her cup on the side table, she pulled her laptop onto her lap and turned it on. In a few minutes, she was into her story, back inside her characters' heads, and acting out first one scene, then another. Followed by third.

She reached for her coffee to take a sip. Cold.

Rising out of her characters' worlds, she set the laptop on the ottoman and grasped her coffee mug. She made her way into the kitchen thinking about where those characters were going next, poured the hot coffee, and stood holding the beverage in both hands, looking out the window lost in thought.

Working out the scene in her mind, she pondered calling Mary Lou. She'd become dependent on her lately when it came to the book. Mary Lou Picketts was a professional book editor. Sometimes she called herself a book doctor. She had a great listening ear and gave solid direction. She'd been coaching Katie about following her gut more when she was writing. To lighten up on some of the rules and let her voice and her own writing style shine through. Katie listened back. As much of a carefree rule-breaker she was in her personal life, she'd grabbed on to the grammar and sentence-structure rules of her English professors in college and found a safety net in making her passages clean, tight, and grammatically correct.

A few weeks ago, when Mary was in the library doing some research, she and Katie started chatting, and before Katie knew it, Mary had offered to read and give her some pointers on her book.

Katie was sure Mary was going to love the story.

Mary returned the half-written, dog-eared and bleeding profusely hard copy of the manuscript with a frown.

"I do love the story line and your characters, Katie," she said. "But there is so much that needs work to get this sold in New York. The good news is I can help you."

Katie stared. "Really?"

Nodding, Mary added, "It's simple, really Katie. You need to trust your gut more. I'm not hearing your voice yet."

"What? Are you sure?"

"Oh yes. I'm sure. What I'm reading is stiff prose. You need to put the life back into it."

Katie was stunned. "But I've worked and worked to make sure that every sentence and every paragraph is concise and clear and..."

"And all of the i's are dotted and the t's are crossed. Boring."

Shocked, Katie stared back at Mary. "I don't understand."

Mary thumbed through the manuscript. "Look, Katie. I've known you since grade school. We were never friends because we were opposite ends of the spectrum when it came to popularity. In fact, back then, if I thought we had books in common, I would have been amazed. You were gregarious and expressive and fun. You took risks and didn't let grass grow under your feet. You still don't. But your prose? Well, it reads like a sample in an English book, like sentences ready to diagram. No life. No passion. Reflect your personality in your writing, Katie. Be haphazard and unpredictable sometimes. Heck, drop in a sentence fragment once in a while, especially in dialogue. Your dialogue is rather stilted."

"Stilted? A sentence fragment? Seriously?"

Mary grinned. "Yes. Be a risk taker with your words. I promise it will be fine."

Katie stared at her, processing the information. Finally, she said, "You've just undone everything I was taught about writing. I don't know where to start first."

Sighing, Mary grasped her hand. "No worries and don't panic. The good part is you have a fantastic and fresh story line, *and* you know the rules. Now you need to learn how to break the rules intentionally. We'll get there."

Katie was still reeling. "Really?"

"Yes, and stop using semi-colons in dialogue. People don't talk in semi-colons!"

It wasn't an easy afternoon for her but over time, all of Mary's advice sunk in. Since that day, Katie had been rewriting and Mary had been reading, and they had become friends. Even though Mary's initial critique was a little difficult to swallow, Katie knew the story would be better because of it.

She was finding the balance in her writing and her voice, according to Mary, was beginning to shine through. She wondered how the three scenes she'd written this morning would measure up. Perhaps she would email them off to her to find out.

She stared out the window at the backyard a little longer,

imagining Grammy wandering about in her nightgown trimming her roses. She smiled. Grammy was a risk taker in all parts of her life but she had definitely found harmony and balance. Her worlds had collided when she meant Grandpa, Grammy had told her once, and her free spirit hippy days of her youth had meshed with the conservative banker's personality of her husband. They were happy together until the end.

Balance. Maybe that's what she needed. Often it seemed whether in her writing, or in her personal life, it was either all or nothing. No in-between. Could she find the in-between and the balance in both? Mary was already helping her see that she didn't need to be so rigid in her writing. She could break the writing rules once she knew and understood the writing rules—and broke them to her advantage.

Could she break her own relationship rules in real life? Could she find the balance between having her dream and having Chris too? That was really what she was afraid of, wasn't it?

BEFORE HE KNEW IT, Chris was sitting in Suzie's kitchen at *Sweet Hart Inn*, chatting over cinnamon coffee and blueberry muffins. Suzie took in the conversation, glancing back and forth between Chris and Matt, as Matt explained why they were there and told her of Chris' dilemma. Suzie sure didn't look like a matchmaker to him.

What the hell. Matchmaker? Aren't those people only in books, or in Broadway plays, or in Ireland or something?

While Matt did most of the talking, Chris nodded occasionally and agreed. Suzie took it all in. She bit her lip, frowned now and again, and even grimaced once or twice.

Finally, she added her two cents. "My work is cut out for me. I need to think about this."

"Can you help?" Matt asked.

She nodded. "Absolutely. I first need to consider the approach."

"Approach?" Chris shook his head. "How about hog-tying and throttling her?"

Suzie's left eyebrow shot up, and she leaned forward. "Look here, Chris Marks. I don't know you that well, you being fairly new in town and all, but I do know Katie Long and that girl won't take to being treated as chattel." She sat back in her chair and eyed him another second. Or two.

Chris bristled a little. "Suzie, I've lived here for two years, and you see me several times a week at the bakery. You know me."

She leaned in. "Not like I know other people around here, whose families have had their roots in this town for generations. Two years is nothing, Chris, when you live in a small town."

That again. How could he forget? He figured she was right. He was always amazed at the inner workings of this small community. "I get it. So now what?"

Suzie ignored him and continued. "I trust my brother-in-law here. He thinks you have potential and says you love her, so I'm thinking we can work together." She paused and eyed him.

Chris was almost afraid to move or take a breath. He started to say something then shut his mouth again as Suzie tapped her manicured fingertips on the tabletop.

"Now Katie?" she started again, "She grew up here then went away to college and didn't come back until recently. Always was a little spitfire but smart as a tack. Runs in the family. That grandmother of hers was a pistol. I never thought Katie would settle down although I do have my hopes that you could be the man. I'm an old school type of person who thinks that everyone needs a partner, so I believe in love and happily-ever-afters. I think you have a chance with her. I simply think you have been going about it the wrong way."

He'd had about enough talk and stood. "Suzie, I appreciate your involvement, but I know how to handle Katie Marie Long. I've been handling her..."

"With kid gloves?"

"Um, no."

"Buying her roses?"

"Well, not lately."

"Picnic at the lake?"

"Not really our thing."

"Take her out for a fancy dinner in Asheville?"

"No, but we get take-out from the BBQ Hut every Friday night."

Suzie crinkled her nose and scoffed. "Ever bought her chocolate? Perfume?"

He thought briefly about the red silk gown he'd had delivered to her house last night but figured he'd struck out on that chord too. Katie had not even acknowledged that it had arrived. He shook his head.

"A fancy pink rabbit-eared vibrator?" Suzie questioned, staring a hole through him.

Chris felt his eyes grow wide. "No. With me around she has no need for a dil—."

Suzie put her hand up and stood. "Don't go there." Pausing, she squinted. "Hey, you know I witnessed what happened a few days ago, remember?"

"What?"

She stepped closer. For a moment, he thought she might grasp his chin and turn his face from side to side. "You know, across from the church?"

He gave her a slow nod.

"You and Katie were arguing. The day Nash came to

rescue Mary from her wedding. I saw her red car peel out of your driveway. She was saying something like…"

Chris interrupted. "It will be a cold day in hell before I marry the likes of you." That statement rang through his head for days.

Suzie exhaled and he did the same. Then she pulled herself up to her full five-foot-and inches-to-spare height and said, "We'll see about that." Glancing at Matt, she added, "I know what I need to do. Go spruce him up and have him back here at ten minutes of seven. Don't be late and come in the back door."

She scrambled off, grasped her cell phone from the counter, and dialed while muttering to herself.

Matt shrugged and grinned. "So, we're gonna do what she says. Believe me. Crossing the women in this family is a big mistake."

"*This* is all a big mistake. I can take care of my own problems, and I don't need a damn matchmaker."

Chuckling, Matt continued. "Of course you don't. That's why Katie is running away from you." He glanced at his watch. "We've got nine hours. You need a haircut. Probably have to go to Asheville. Maybe a suit. I'd say roses would be good, too."

"This is gonna cost me."

Matt snickered. "She worth it?"

"Yeah. Shit."

Chapter Five

How she ended up here, sitting at a fancy-set table in Suzie Hart Matthew's dining room, when she had planned to nerd out all day with her writing, Katie wasn't certain. Well, of course, she knew the sequence of events, but it was so far removed from her plan for the day that she had to give herself a mental double take. And for some reason, now, she was feeling a little uneasy. Had she allowed herself to be suckered into something that would turn around and bite her in the ass?

When Suzie called earlier, insisting that she come to the book club and contribute to the discussion on that new memoir by Gabby Mortimer, she'd been puzzled. She'd been deep into writing scene five when her cell phone rang. She answered. "Suzie?"

"Oh Katie, good. So glad you answered. Look, I'm having an impromptu book discussion over here tonight. Evidently, this new book is all the rage, and the ladies want to continue the discussion tonight. Grace couldn't have it over at *Romantically Yours* because of Izzie's scout's cookie drive and I wondered if you could come. The ladies and I think you would be a great addition to the club, being a librarian and all."

Book club? She'd heard about the club over at Grace's gift shop. Suzie's cousin owned the eclectic boutique across the street from the library. Since she'd been back in town, Katie had popped in a couple of times to buy cards or candles but had yet to experience the book club. A gregarious older group of women, they sometimes moved the meeting to Friday nights at Rick's Café next door to Grace's shop, starting the discussion with happy hour. Katie thought them a closed group of friends who used books as an excuse to drink wine and dollar margaritas. "Oh, Suzie, thank you for thinking of me but no. I have plans for today." And she did.

But Suzie wasn't about to be deterred. She went on to say the Mortimer book, *One Step, Two Step,* was trending on Twitter. Katie knew nothing about that or the book. Suzie shared how the book told the story of Gabby's travels through Asia after her husband died from pancreatic cancer. Then how she had lived three years with Monks in Indonesia, after which she adopted a little girl from Thailand who was suffering from some rare bone disease that made her bow-legged. And then, she told of the struggle of bringing the girl back to the states, only to be discriminated against by her neighbors in her white-collar, gated golf community.

Katie wasn't certain that it was the kind of memoir she wanted to read, let alone discuss, and wondered, briefly, if there even was such a book. She had never heard of Gabby Mortimer. She didn't even know if there were Monks in Indonesia, but Suzie insisted that the book was an up-and-coming bestseller and all the rage. Her editor had told her so. Not that Suzie's cookbook editor would know diddlysquat about bestselling memoirs, even if it were published with the same house.

If Katie hadn't been so busy working on her own novel,

she might have run out and checked the library catalog before heading to Suzie's to see what the heck Suzie was talking about or at least Googled the author or title. But she didn't. She'd been too engrossed in her story. And it had been a while since she'd been able to let herself do that.

"Suzie, no. I'm..." She started to make up an excuse for what she was doing. The whole town didn't need to know that she was writing, did they? But then she thought, well, she'd take a risk. "I'm writing today."

There was a slight pause from the other end. "Writing? Do you write, Katie?"

She took a breath and steadied herself. "Yes. I'm working on a novel."

"Oh, my goodness, that's perfect! Maybe you can tell us about it when you come. Mary Lou is going to be here too, and I'm sure all of the book club ladies will be excited to learn all about it! So be here at six thirty. Okay? I have snacks and liquor, so no need to bring anything. Bye!"

In typical Suzie fashion, she was gone.

Katie hadn't actually agreed but now that Suzie was expecting her, she decided to go with the flow. Be good to get out of the house, she told herself. Right? Socialize. And talk about books. Books were her favorite thing, after all. Well, right after sex. And with no sex this weekend, books were a good substitute.

Sort of.

She *had* looked forward to it. Earlier. But glancing about now, Katie affirmed her earlier suspicions. No book discussion was about to happen here this evening.

The dining room table was set for seduction, not stimulating intellectual discussion. Two place settings of fine bone China, sparkling crystal water and wine glasses, and polished silver reflected flickering candlelight. A lazy tune played soft in the background. The lights were low. Rose petals sprinkled on the expensive white linen tablecloth balanced the strawberries dipped in dark chocolate perched on a cake stand in the center of the table.

The song changed and like an idiot, she hummed along. *Ta-ta-ta. Ta-ta-ta. Ta-ta-TA-DA. Ta-ta-TA-DA. Ta-ta-TA-DA. Matchmaker, matchmaker, make me a match and...*

Matchmaker. Crap. She'd heard the rumors about Suzie.

I'm an idiot.

I. Will. Kill. Him.

"Wine?"

Suzie sashayed in holding a bottle of red. She smiled and gravitated toward one of the glasses and poured a small amount. Picking the goblet up by the stem, she handed it to Katie.

"It's from New Zealand. Fruity. Goes nicely with the berries and chocolate. I think I'll add this combo to my cookbook, *Perfectly Matched*. What do you think?"

Katie squinted, took the glass, and thought about downing the wine with one gulp, then remembered she shouldn't be drinking. "I think you're up to something." She handed the glass back to her host. "There is no book club going on here tonight. Where is he?"

Wrinkling her nose, Suzie took back the wine. A timer went off in the kitchen. "Oh," she said then. "Make yourself at home. I'll be right back."

It was like she blinked her eyes and disappeared.

"Witch."

Exhaling, Katie reached for the wine, brought it to her lips, and paused. Firmly, she set it down again. "Dammit."

She stood and whirled, ready to escape, but something solid and unmoving and male blocked her way.

Chest. And she barreled right into it.

Chris steadied her, fingers gripping her biceps. "Going somewhere?"

With an exhale long and deep enough to force out any frustration left in her body, she stepped back and pushed away. As she opened her mouth to blast him for whatever little scenario he had gone and paid too much for, she clamped it back closed again.

Whoa. What the hell?

"Uh. Oh. Um. Wow." Damn he looked good.

The suit was crisp and new. Deep chocolate brown. Underneath the jacket, he wore a starched ivory shirt graced with a necktie the color of a mocha latte. Her gaze rose to his face. He'd shaved. Close. Every hair was in place. And his deep-set amber eyes twinkled.

He'd gone to a lot of trouble here. For her.

Not to mention he smelled like pure lust. She leaned forward and inhaled. Deep. No. Musk. *Oh. My.*

"Oh Chris. What have you done?" She gritted her teeth and challenged herself not to get caught up in this mess. But he was good. Oh, yes. He was damn good. And so was Suzie.

Criminy.

Chris ambled to the table, glanced back at her once, and plucked a dipped strawberry off the cake plate. "Hungry?"

She pursed her lips. He moved closer and dangled the berry in front of her face. She watched his eyes, crinkled at the corners, and chewed her bottom lip.

"Come bite me," he teased, waving the succulent fruit in front of her. Then he tilted his head back, opened his mouth, and slowly sucked the chocolate off that strawberry while she watched.

"Damn you."

He laughed. "Want one? I'll feed you."

"No."

"Sure, you do. I can see it in your eyes."

"I don't want one."

"What if I rub it over your—"

"Stop it!"

"Then lick off the excess juices—"

"Enough."

"Wanna bite something else then?"

Okay. Time to leave. Sex was sex was sex...and she'd always been able to resist when it wasn't in her best interest. And sex with Chris right now was definitely not in her best interest but the man was relentless. This time, however, she would not fold. Would not succumb. Would not give in no matter what he did or said or...

"Or I could bite you."

Shit. She literally quivered between her legs. God, she was wet already. She backed away. "Chris, look..." Talking was not working. She needed action.

Retreat. *Retreat!*

Unfortunately, he was a step ahead of her. Grasping both her forearms, he hauled her up against him. It was good. Yes. Good to be next to him.

Why couldn't she just give in? Why was she fighting this? Her feelings were real. Genuine. She loved him, she knew it in her heart. Why couldn't she cave? And he was so irresistible when it came to sex....

His lips found her ear, and he nuzzled. "Katie, I've missed you so."

They swayed and her chest grew warm, swelling with the wings of a thousand butterflies that were frantic for release. To fly free and to live and love and...

Butterflies died when they mated, right?

His tongue traced the shell of her ear. Made slow, lazy, tempting circles. Groaning, she slid her hands around his waist, under his jacket, felt the muscles over his ribs. "You bastard," she breathed.

"I love you, Katie. Please, let's talk about this."

His words were soft-spoken and sincere. She knew he

loved her. Still... "Not yet, Chris. This just feels so impossible...."

Both of his arms went around her shoulders then. His mouth embarked on a slow, lazy trail down her neck. "Nothing is impossible, sweetheart. Let's talk. Suzie has made this great dinner, and she has a room ready upstairs that we can stay in tonight." His hands worked their way up her neck and cradled her face. "And talk this out. It's the right thing. For us. Me. You. The baby..."

The baby.

Tears stung the backs of her eyelids again.

The baby.

If it weren't for *the baby*, he wouldn't have asked her to marry him. And she wouldn't be thinking about it, either. Because she had other plans. Other ways she wanted to live her life. A baby wasn't in the plans.

Even though the idea of a baby was beginning to grow on her.

But she had dreams. She hadn't wanted to be stuck at home with a baby. Not like her mother, who died before she lived out her life.

No.

Except the damned condom broke. *Sonofabitch.* And she'd switched doctors with the move and had been off the pill for a month or so. *Stupid.*

She pushed away. Broke the embrace. Fell back two more steps.

Her eyes filled with tears and she cursed herself. Damned hormones! She couldn't even look at a kid anymore without crying. Then she leveled her gaze on Chris' face and stared straight into his eyes.

"No, Chris. It's not going to work. All of this..." She waved her hand toward the table. "...this seduction scene won't help to convince me. I won't marry you. You'll be sorry in the long run. I'm not going to ruin your life. Or mine. Or the baby's."

She knew that made no sense. But he'd confused her and inside her head, everything was muddled. Inside her heart...? She stumbled toward the door. He caught her by the elbow.

"Katie, stop. I don't have a clue what is up with you. What do you mean when you say you'd ruin my life? How in the world...?"

She twisted and jerked her arm out of his grasp. "Just what I said." She could barely hold the sobs back now.

His voice rose. "What the hell, Katie! The baby is coming! Whether you like it or not. We have to figure out something. We have to plan. We can't keep ignoring this and you have to stop pushing me away. Pushing both of us away!"

Whether I like it or not. The baby is coming.

The realization hit her square in the chest, ripping her wide open. Every emotion she'd kept pent up for so long was whooshed out for the world to trample on. For Chris to see. She'd never been so scared in her life.

Pregnant.

Baby.

Hers.

Theirs.

What was she going to do? What were *they* going to do?

Too much. It was all too much. In the next instant, an agonizing sob wrenched from her throat. Then she did what she was good at doing lately.

Run.

She raced past Suzie standing in her living room, tugged at the inside door and threw it back against the wall more aggressively than she had intended, then pushed through the screen door and heard it slap hard as it closed behind her.

She had to get out of there before she totally, and unmistakenly, lost her marbles.

But a cold blast of wind abruptly stopped her on the porch, as snow blew in around her ankles, halting her.

"Shit. Where did this effing snow come from?"

Turning, she raced back inside the house, past Suzie again, and ran up the staircase.

CLOSING his eyes against the scene that had just unfolded before him, Chris's hopes and dreams sank. He had no clue where to turn next. What to do. The only thing he knew was that he couldn't give up. She was carrying his child. He loved her. And he already loved that baby more than anything, too.

Aching inside, he grimaced at the pain. What would he do if he couldn't convince her to marry him? What was it going to take?

At the sound of footsteps, he opened his eyes to find Suzie standing framed by the dining room doorway.

"Didn't go so well, huh?" she asked softly.

He shook his head.

Suzie sighed. "This one has me puzzled."

"Yeah. Like one big old eight-hundred-piece monster."

Nodding, Suzie said, "She's upstairs. I'll go talk to her."

A little hope rose in his chest. Girl talk? Maybe? "It's hard to get her to open up."

"I know. She was three years behind me in school, but I know her about as well as anyone. Let me see what I can do."

"She's pregnant."

Suzie's eyes grew wide.

"It's mine."

"Ah. Important information."

"We just found out. Last weekend."

"Hm. The day I saw you."

"Yes."

"So, it's still new. Emotions are running high."

"Yes."

Suzie nodded. "And hers are cockeyed."

"I don't want to lose her or the baby. And I don't have a clue what I'm doing wrong or what's happening in her head."

She studied him for a moment then reached out and clasped her hand over his. "Go back in the family room with Brad. Have a beer. Relax. Let's see what I can find out."

SOMEONE KNOCKED AT THE DOOR. Great.

Why she hadn't run straight out the front door and through the snow, Katie would never know—but her stomach was turning flip-flops and she thought she was going to be sick. It had happened a few times lately, so she ran up the stairs looking for a bathroom. By chance, she found one that came attached to a bedroom and now, she lay stretched out over a crisp, cool, white cotton comforter in a room painted a soothing shade of blue.

It calmed her. Somewhat. Lying there. Allowing her some time to think. Letting her brain clear. As the door creaked open, she didn't open her eyes.

"Katie, it's me. Suzie."

"I know." She smelled her vanilla perfume.

The weight of Suzie's small frame settled on the bed. "Lots of stuff going on, huh?"

Katie snorted.

"He loves you."

"I know."

"He's a good man."

"I know that, too."

"Then what is the problem?"

Silence. She turned her head into the pillow.

"I like to be spanked." Her words were muffled.

"Oh. Hm. Really."

Katie could tell by the tone of her voice that Suzie was trying to be dignified. "Yes."

"I'm not quite sure what that has to do with all of this, but I'm intrigued."

Sitting up, Katie looked straight at Suzie. "Is that the kind of mother a baby should have? One who likes to be spanked? One who likes to screw her boyfriend on the side of the road in the middle of the night? One who doesn't wear panties and wishes her boyfriend would nail her between the stacks on an early Sunday morning while Geraldine Weissmuller is reading the morning paper in the children's section?"

Katie watched Suzie's eyes grow wide. Oh hell.

"Well, Katie Long, babies generally don't much care about any of that. All a baby wants is to be dry and fed and held."

Slapping the bed, Katie exclaimed. "See? That's just it! I don't have time for those things. I don't want to change my lifestyle. I don't want to change the fact that I like to be spanked."

Suzie stared. "Who says you have to?"

Katie blinked. And glared. "Um. I don't know. It just feels like a mom should..."

Grasping her hands, Suzie shook her. Katie looked down at the grip she had on her. "Katie look," Suzie began. "You're afraid of something here and guess what, that's pretty much normal. No woman wants her life to change when she gets married or has a baby but it will a little. That doesn't mean you have to stop your sex life."

Katie swallowed. "Well, I hope not but things change."

"Not if you don't want them to."

"But most women tell me that—"

Suzie held up a hand. "Okay, that's enough. Stay right here I'll be right back."

Katie watched as Suzie skittered off out the door and down the hall, then back again. She tossed some things on the bed—a blindfold, several silk scarves, and a garter belt. Katie took the objects in and glanced back up into Suzie's face.

"...and your point is?"

Suzie sighed. "I also have black leather boots and a bustier in the bedroom and other toys. Look, Katie, I am a mom and I still have a helluva lot of fun in the bedroom."

Katie thought about that. "I suppose I'm being stupid."

"No, you are trying to figure out things."

"Suzie, I know partly what this is. I don't want to make this decision. About the baby. About us. I want... This may sound weird, but I want Chris to just take over and make the decisions."

Suzie's brows knit. "Sounds to me like he already has. He loves you, Katie, and wants to be with you. To marry you."

"I know, I know. But I don't want him to ask me, I want him to tell me."

Suzie smirked. "Tell you."

"Yes. He needs to like...*order* me to marry him."

"Order you?"

"Yeah. Insist. Demand it. Not give me a choice in the matter. Tell me I'm his, that he owns me, that he will make all of my decisions. Hell, that he owns my orgasms. Whatever. I need for him to take damn control."

Katie watched Suzie's face turn squishy.

"That doesn't sound like you," she finally said.

"I *know*. But it is what I need. I don't want to make *this* decision. I mean, I want to, and I don't want to. I'm..." She whooshed out a breath. "Oh, hell. I hope you don't think badly of me or anything, but..." She glimpsed again into Suzie's face and the words came tumbling out. "You see, the thing is this—I like it when Chris takes control. During sex, particularly. It works well for us. When I'm, well, you know, submissive a little."

She watched Suzie's nostril's flair. "Well, what do you know?"

"Are you shocked?"

Suzie shook her head. "Not really. Brad and I play but we don't get seriously into the control issues. I've read about these things. You know that erotic trilogy that was so popular for a while, with movies and everything, that all the woman talked about? Well, I read all three of the books and I sort of get this. It's powerful to give up the power."

"Oh shit. It's not really like that. It's different. I just, just..."

"Just what, Katie?"

"I've been the bad girl for a long time. I need for Chris to make me his and take the bad girl out of me, in a way. I need to be punished. And I need for him to do it over and over and over again...."

"Oh!"

"I know what you are thinking."

"I'm not sure you do. I get you don't want to make the decision, but will you be happy with what he decides?"

Would she? Katie thought back to a conversation she had with Grammy when she was in high school. *I swear, if that grandpa of yours hadn't taken the upper hand and told me I was marrying him, whether I liked it or not, I probably never would have. And I would have missed out on a whole lot of life. Like you, Katie Marie.*

"Yes. I need him to do this. I was always the hardheaded kid in school, the control freak, had to have my way... And that was fine. Then. But the thing is this. I'm still hard-head-ed." Then the rest of everything that was on her mind all came tumbling out. "I have a dream, Suzie. I want to be an author. I want a New York publisher. I want to see my book on the shelves of the Harbor Falls library. And I've had this dream for so long that my hard-headed self can't let it go."

Suzie looked puzzled. "Okay. I get all of that. But I don't see how Chris and a baby will interfere with your dreams, Katie. Don't let that happen!"

"I know that in my heart, but my head tells me that with the baby on the way my dream isn't going to happen. Not in New York. Not if I am married to Chris. Not if I'm a mom. Although, marrying him isn't the issue, is it? Because the baby is coming whether I marry him or not. I'm so confused! See why I need for him to do this!"

Suzie gave her hand a squeeze. "Honey, we all get confused in times like these. And your hormones are running amok, I can tell that. But give Chris a chance. I'm sure if you talk with him—"

"No! I can't talk to him about it. He came here because he wanted to live in a small town. I've been trying to get out of it forever. Been scheming and planning my way since high school. I lived away for ten years and now I'm back—but I did that so I could save money and write the book, and then move again. I've been plotting and planning forever, and Suzie, I don't know how to stop. I don't know how to let go of the dream. And I don't know how to tell Chris about it. That's why—"

She paused.

"That's why what, Katie?"

"That is why I need for him to take control. Not only in the bedroom. But of me. My life. Our life."

Suzie eyed her. "But what if it backfires?"

Katie stared at her. "How? What do you mean?"

"What if he orders you to marry him and you haven't got this baby phobia and dream-crashing notion out of your head yet and you start to resent him for it?"

Blowing out a breath, Katie felt the tears popping up in

her eyes again. "Oh shit. I didn't think of that. I wouldn't. I mean, I'm *choosing* for him to do this. Right?" She stopped talking and bit her lip. "Do you really think I have baby phobia?"

"What would you call it?"

She shook her head. "I don't know."

Suzie squeezed her hands again. "Have you really never shared your dreams with Chris?"

Horrified, Katie sat straight up in the bed. "No! Never. And don't you go telling him either!"

"Katie, I wouldn't. That is your story to tell."

She deflated again to the bed, her head on the pillow. "I *want* to give up the dream. For him. For us. For the baby. I'm not sure how to do it on my own. Not sure how to tell him."

Suzie exhaled. "Katie, don't give anything up. You don't have to."

Leaning up again, she said, "But I do! Don't you see?"

"No, I don't." Suzie narrowed her gaze, then said under her breath, "Hog-tied and throttled."

"Excuse me?"

"Damn. He knew all along."

Katie wasn't sure what that meant.

Standing, Suzie said firmly, "Katie Marie Long, you are staying the night. Slip those clothes off and get between the sheets. I'm having a talk with Chris and then I am sending him on his way. And you, Missy, are going to get a good night's sleep. In the morning, I'm going to feed you an excellent breakfast because tomorrow, your life is going to change forever."

Katie didn't even flinch or question as Suzie left the room. She just did as she was told. That was easy.

Chapter Six

"Chris Marks, I have the answer to your prayers."

Looking up, Chris wondered if the two beers he'd just drank with Suzie's husband, Brad, were making him see things. What in the world was Suzie carrying in here?

"You were right," she told him. "You do know the best way to handle her."

Standing, he looked again at the objects in her hands.

"Yes, you are seeing correctly. Roses, strawberries, or picnics by the lake will not woo Katie Long. She's a bit of a different breed and you knew that all along. What you need, what *she* needs, are these two things. Maybe more but we'll start here. The palm of your hand wouldn't hurt either."

She extended both arms and he blinked, clearly seeing the items. He thought he heard Brad snicker from the sidelines. From the fingers of Suzie's left hand dangled a pair of black leather handcuffs. In the right, she gripped one very fine and leather spanking paddle.

"Katie needs you to take control of the situation and her life. Your life together. She avoids talking to you about it because she doesn't know *how* to talk about it, and she doesn't know how to *accept* what you are asking her to do. Don't ask, Chris. Tell. Tell her what is going to happen, that you are getting married, that you are going to have a baby, and that you are going to be a happy family together. And above all else, tell her that you have no intentions of ever stopping using either of these items—or other closely related items on her— and make that woman yours. Tell her that *nothing* about your relationship will change. Nothing, and that includes your sex life. I guarantee you she will be putty in your hands if you play your cards right. Hog-tied and throttled is exactly what she needs."

She thrust the objects toward him. "Now take these and use them. If you aren't sure how then I will leave you two boys alone for a while." She winked. "Brad can give you some pointers."

Turning on her heel, she made her way out of the living room and toward the kitchen. Chris looked down at the objects in his hands, then to Brad. "Well, I'll be damned. Your wife is good."

Brad winked. "You have no idea."

THE NEXT MORNING, Katie pushed back an empty plate which moments earlier had held eggs, sausage, biscuits and gravy, and a healthy scoop of hash brown casserole. "I am not going to be able to eat for a week," she exclaimed, glancing to both Suzie and Brad. "Tell me you don't eat like this every morning."

Smiling, Suzie rose and reached for hers and Brad's plates. "Oh, heck no, Katie. Just when we have guests or company."

"Which is pretty much most of the time lately," Brad added. "This is a rare morning we aren't serving breakfast for at least six or seven people." He pushed back from the table and stood. "Speaking of which, we have a tour bus checking in at the lodge in about an hour. I need to get up the hill."

Leaning into him, Suzie lifted her face for a quick kiss. Brad gave her a hug and a peck on her lips, then smiling down said, "I'll see you later today. Have a good morning, sweetheart."

Suzie beamed and watched him leave.

"That was sickening sweet," Katie said, as Suzie turned back. "And really lovely. You two are quite the couple."

Shrugging, Suzie stepped away from the table. "It took us a while to get here but things are good. Besides, he likes my cooking." She grinned and headed toward the kitchen.

"I would weigh four hundred pounds eating like this!" Katie stood and lifted her plate, following Suzie. "But thank you, the food was awesome."

"My pleasure. It's what I love to do."

Katie followed her into the kitchen, and they chattered about this and that while cleaning up. Although Suzie was a little older, Katie wondered why they weren't good friends. Three years in age makes a big difference when you are kids, she guessed, and then there was high school and college and working in Charlotte after that—all different sorts of challenges.

But she liked Suzie and grinned right now as she listened to her talk about her new cookbook. While they were cleaning up, a surprising call had come from her agent and Suzie learned there was talk of a television show. Not local but on a famous food channel, no less, and based in New York City. Suzie danced around the kitchen in excitement all morning since she'd heard the news.

Hard-pressed not to be excited for her, Katie came to a sudden realization. Suzie was actually living her dream. "You are amazing," she told her.

"How so?"

"Just look at you," Katie began. "You're married, you have the inn, you write cookbooks, and now you may have your own television show. In addition, you have a child and husband. You have made your dreams happen despite it all. You know how incredible that is? The odds are largely stacked against that happening."

Suzie glanced her way. "It isn't always easy, Katie. In fact, sometimes it is damn hard work but when you want something, you keep working at it. I don't think I can give up."

Nodding, Katie thought she was beginning to understand. "I've been selling myself short."

Suzie waited a minute before responding. "Perhaps. Do you think so?"

"I do."

"Sometimes we just need a change in perspective."

"And maybe sometimes we need a nudge in the right direction."

"Nudges never hurt." Suzie smiled then turned her attention back to the dishwasher. Katie fell silent and watched her, thinking. After a moment, Suzie turned. "Let's get out of here," she said. "I have something I want to show you downtown. You up for it?"

Katie figured why not? "Sure."

Fifteen minutes later, Suzie parked her Honda Element in front of The Purple Pelican Baby Boutique. Katie tossed her a glance and then silently exited the car when Suzie did. Not saying anything, and thinking even less, she followed her new friend to the front door of the shop and inside.

"Suzie!"

A woman at the back of the called out and turned their way, her mane of long dark hair swinging as she did. She moved between racks and shelves of tiny clothing to reach her friend. "How are you?"

Moving forward to meet her, Suzie hugged the woman.

"Marnie, it's so good to see you. Been too long." Turning, she added, "Meet my friend, Katie Long."

Katie smiled and pushed out her hand. Marnie bypassed the offer and reached in for a hug. Katie was a bit surprised at the bear hug she got back, but managed to reciprocate. Katie generally wasn't much of a hugger. "Nice to meet you, Marnie," she said, pulling away to look into the woman's face.

She was pretty, and maybe a little bit older than Katie had originally thought, with a few crinkles around her bright green eyes and her lips—but her smile and friendly face showed no evidence of age whatsoever.

"Marnie married Greg Malone," Suzie told her. "You know, from high school? He now coaches the high school football team."

Katie knew exactly who Greg Malone was. "Of course! Wow. I didn't know he had married. It's great to meet you, Marnie." She smiled.

"He was not one to be saddled down too early in life with a wife, you know," Marnie said. "I got him after his pro football career and after all of those other women—who had attempted to harness him—wore him down. By the time he got to me," she paused and laughed, her eyes dancing, "he was mine for the picking."

"Oh poo." Suzie batted her hand in the air. "That man fell for you the moment he laid eyes on you, Marnie Malone. And he didn't go kicking and screaming either. One look at you, and he knew he was a goner. Told me so himself."

"Well, you would be the one he would tell, seeing that you were such good friends growing up."

Suzie nodded. "He better. Greg is like a brother to me. But reminiscing is not why we are here, Marnie. Can you show us around? I'd like for Katie to take a stroll through your shop, if you don't mind."

The focus then turned to Katie, and she felt a little uncomfortable. "I, um…"

"Are you expecting, Katie?"

"Well, um…"

Marnie gave Suzie a glance. Their gazes exchanged a private moment, and Katie could read between the lines. "Suzie, you don't have to do this. I will figure this out."

"Nothing to figure out, darling, you're pregnant and that's a fact. Now, let's go explore the cute baby things and see if we can get you past this baby phobia of yours."

Marnie's eyes lit up. "Baby phobia? Is there such a thing?"

Suzie sighed. "Apparently." She hooked an arm with Katie's. "C'mon, let's let Marnie show us around the place."

Before she knew it, Katie Marie Long was lost in baby land and loving it. For the first time since she'd heard the awful news, the news wasn't so awful anymore. She was actually, almost, nearly, excited.

CHRIS sure as hell hoped he could pull this off. With props from Suzie and tips from Brad, he was sure he had everything under control—but Katie was unpredictable. Lately even more so. How would she react?

He paced the bedroom. The scene was set. Nothing too fancy, just the basics. Later, if things went well, he'd bring up the wine chilling downstairs and the cheeseboard in the fridge, and the dirty movies on DVD he'd brought from home.

He hoped to hell all of this worked.

Suzie's voice was in his ear with last-minute instructions. And as much as he didn't want anyone else in the room with him at this moment, he let the conversation tick through his head one more time. He wanted to be certain he was doing the right thing. He couldn't afford to screw up at this point.

Here is the plan, she said.

Plan?

Make her yours—you know how—then ask her about her dreams.

What? She has dreams?

Yes, dammit, and if you'd asked her about them before this, you might know already. So use the "props" as you will, provide her with pleasure upon pleasure until you are both spent, then order her to marry you, and finally, be sure to ask her about her dreams. That's the most important part. Don't forget. Do it.

Do it. He had to do it.

You have to take control of this. Get what you want. It is what she wants, too. Trust me.

He hoped to hell Suzie was right. Inside his gut hurt right now, and he wasn't so certain.

Maybe that was just hope afraid to come out. Maybe he had worried himself sick too much that he was *afraid* to hope.

He sat on the edge of the bed and exhaled with a nervous whoosh. "This has to work," he whispered. "Please, let this work."

Chapter Seven

"I can't wait to tell Brad!"

Suzie was talking about the television show again. After leaving The Purple Pelican, she had asked Katie if it was okay if they drove up to the lodge to tell Brad the news and drop off something to a guest.

"Of course. It will be fun," she told her. Katie was happy for Suzie and loved the way she and Brad were so supportive of each other and was happy to tag along. Besides, Katie needed some fresh air and perspective. After a night of deep sleep and that monstrous breakfast, followed by an hour of baby oohing and ahing, her brain was still fuzzy and adjusting to everything. Mountain air was always good to clear the fog.

Would Chris be supportive of her dreams, like Brad was of Suzie's?

Suzie rattled on while ambling along the mountain road. Katie heard most of it, trying to keep her mind off Chris and... well, off the semi-embarrassing and personal things Katie had said last night to Suzie.

How could she have shared her intimate sexual secrets? She didn't talk about sex much with other women. That was part of the mystery about who she was, in part. The other part was that sex was private, and she didn't like chatting about her escapades over morning coffee or a glass of wine. Thinking about what she'd said to Suzie last night made her tummy twist. Thankfully, there had been no mention of it this morning.

Leaning back in the seat, she closed her eyes. The day was crisp and new and the further they moseyed up the mountain, the more serene the surroundings and calmer her heart became. She cracked her passenger window a little for some fresh air—sweet pines tickled her nose and the rush of a brook comforted her ear.

"So, is that all right with you?"

Katie tilted forward and looked at Suzie. Had she slept?

"I'm sorry. What did you say?"

"I said..." But Katie didn't hear the end of her sentence. Outside Suzie's window, she saw the Lodge roll by.

"We passed the Lodge."

"Yes, that's what I said."

"Huh?"

"I need to run something out to a guest in one of the cabins."

Katie settled back into her seat. She had dozed, she guessed. "Oh, that's fine. I'm just your sidekick today. I'm glad I don't have to work today since it's a holiday."

Suzie grinned and drove on. In another five minutes, they pulled onto a dirt road and rambled toward the last cabin. She parked and looked ahead. "I don't see their car. Hm."

"Maybe they left for a little while?"

"No, I talked to them this morning. They said they'd be here."

"Maybe they parked out back."

"Yes. Maybe. Would you go knock on the door while I get the stuff out?"

Katie was glad to help. "Sure." She lifted the latch and left the car. Shivering a little against the mountain chill, she pulled the sweater she had borrowed from Suzie earlier that morning snug around her body. Suzie got out of the opposite side and left the engine idling.

As Katie's foot hit the top porch step, she heard the car door slam behind her, the engine gun, and the crunch of wheels on rocks and dirt. Briskly turning, she caught sight of Suzie's orange Honda Element heading down the dirt road in a cloud of dust.

"What the heck?"

Behind her, porch floorboards creaked, and something slapped onto her right wrist. She stiffened and a deep male voice said softly, "Shh, sweetheart. Don't turn around. Don't say a word. And do exactly as I say."

Chris. *Oh, hell's bells.*

The next five minutes blurred by in a nano-second. He lifted and carried her upstairs, stripped her naked, and secured her to the four-poster bed with leather restraints before she could protest.

Although she did protest. A little.

"What do you think you are doing?"

"Making you come to your senses."

"I know my senses, and they are just fine. Let me go, you bastard."

"Not a chance, Sweet Pea. Your ass is mine. Tonight, and forever."

"You can't hog-tie me and..." *Shit.* She got it.

Oh, damn. *Damn!* Bless your ever-loving, matchmaking heart, Ms. Suzie Hart! Katie trembled a little inside at the anticipation of what was to come. Apparently, Suzie hadn't forgotten what she'd told her last night and *apparently*, she had somehow communicated those private needs and desires of hers to Chris.

Apparently!

She strained against the leather restraints and eyeballed the cuffs on her wrists. She watched as Chris pulled out a leather paddle from behind his back and straight away, she started breathing heavier.

"Oh. Yes."

~

LOOKING DOWN at Katie's wild and wide eyes, Chris suddenly had second thoughts. He put one knee on the bed and laid the paddle down. "Katie, I'm sorry. This is a mistake. I don't want to do anything to hurt you or anything that you don't want to do, and..."

She glared at him and jerked forward, her lips pressed tightly together and her nostrils flared. The look on her face was reminiscent of something he'd seen in some horror movie with a possessed heroine.

If her head started spinning....

"Chris Marks," she spit out, "you are not going to hurt me. And if you wuss out on me and uncuff me, I will make you pay for the rest of your life. Do you understand? And the way I will make you pay is by not marrying you. Get it? Do I have to spell it out? Now, dammit, do what you set out to do. And do it now!"

Then she collapsed back against the pillows and exhaled. "Please. Sir!"

Stunned, but jolted to his senses, he grasped the paddle and stood upright, trying to still his panicking heart. Goddamn, would it not stop beating so fast? "Yes, ma'am," he said coolly, moving to the side of the bed and snapping the paddle in his palm. Then he bent to whisper in her ear. "But let's get one thing straight. That's the last "Yes, ma'am" you're going to get from me. I'm the boss. Not you. And that is the last order you will utter for the next twenty-four hours. Do you understand?"

She shuddered and locked her gaze with his. "Yes. Sir."

Heaving in a deep breath, Katie closed her eyes as Chris dragged tip of the paddle over her nipples, then trailed a line down the center of her belly. Her nipples rose to the occasion and hardened. She grasped the chain of the cuff in each of her palms and increased the tension as he straddled her thighs.

Then he stopped.

She peered up at him.

"Are you going to glare at me every time I stop doing something?"

"Perhaps."

"No. No, you will not."

It was at that point he put the blindfold over her eyes. "Ah, much better."

Huffing out another breath, she waited. "What are you doing?"

"You will be quiet."

"Chris, I..."

He placed something on the third finger of her left hand.

"There," he said, "and you don't get to see it until we are finished here."

"What?" She curled toward her hand.

"No use. You can't reach it. Don't even try." Then he added, "Don't take it off. Ever. You understand that? You are mine now."

Something was now tickling between her legs, which immediately distracted her from the other...thing. "Oh..."

"Katie, I need a response to my question."

The tickling again. There. "Wha—?"

"You understand that you never take that ring off your finger, correct? You are mine and you will do as I say. You are marrying me."

Warmth spread all throughout Katie's body. Happy warmth. "Yes, Sir!"

"Good." He scooted off to the side. "Spread your legs for me."

Desire flicked through her. "Spread?"

He flicked the paddle firmly on her outer thigh. She flinched. Then shivered in delight.

"Now. No questions. Spread." The bed shifted with his weight. She did and his palms inched up the insides of her thighs.

"Where's the paddle?" she whispered.

"No questions. We're doing this my way."

"Wha...?"

He kissed her. Right at the juncture of her leg and pelvis. Just a breath away from...

"Oh, yes." She slithered downward and spread wider.

Chris hooked his arms under her legs and tilted her lower body. She felt herself rise a bit.

"Don't move," he whispered, his breath hot against her. "I have you." Dragging his lips along her inner leg, she clenched her thighs and waited. The prickles of his unshaven beard raked along her tender skin. His tongue left a sweet, moist trail toward her lips.

Then he paused.

She waited. Patiently.

For like, eons.

Then she felt the slightest sensation on her clit. First, it was like a breath, followed by the tip of something rough and wet at the same time.

Tickling. Circling.

Moaning, she strained against the cuffs.

The pressure increased as his tongue bore down harder.

Flicked.

Danced.

Sucked.

She jerked and shuddered. "Oh, God."

Chris released her and swooped down, taking her more fully into his mouth. Claiming her for his very own. Laving his tongue over her most tender parts and making sweet love with his tongue.

Her libido swelled from deep inside. Heat gathered under his tongue. Her clit was hard, engorged and erect. Every time he swept his tongue over it, she jerked up and was caught by the restraints.

She would erupt. Knew it. Was so close to exploding. And then he...he....

Stopped.

"Not yet," he breathed. "Not yet."

He moved on top of her.

"Damn you," she uttered and squirmed. His hot body covered hers and she savored the feel of his searing skin. Her body hummed with orgasmic anticipation. He glided along the length of her, his cock branding heat against her hip. "What are you doing?"

"Quiet."

He grasped her right hand and she heard a click. Her hand was free.

Finished? No!

"Turn over."

She lay there.

"Katie, turn over. Now."

Gulping, and twittering deep inside with expectation, she did, laying slightly on her left side and tummy, because of the other cuff.

He straddled her legs, right about the knees.

"You been really bad, disobeying my wishes. Avoiding me."

He flicked the paddle over the fleshy part of ass cheek. The sting both shocked and excited her.

"You've been holding out on me. Making me wait for your answer."

"I know. I didn't mean to upset you. I was so…"

"So what?" He lightly slapped the paddle over her ass again.

"I know. I've been difficult."

"Difficult what?"

"I've been difficult, Sir."

"Yes, you have." He paused for a moment. "But we're coming to an agreement tonight."

Her heart did a little butterfly dance. "Agreement?"

"Yes."

"But what if I…?" The paddle again. This time on the left cheek. Why she craved that sting, she didn't know.

"I know what you want. You just don't know that you want it, too. So, I'll have to take matters into my own hands and convince you."

She squirmed. Waited.

"You *will* marry me, Katie Long. That *is* what you want."

Twitching, she tried to glance over her shoulders, but of course, she still had on the damn blindfold. She wanted to see his face. "I will not."

The sting was slightly more intense this time. Dammit, she was so turned on!

"You will."

"And why should I?"

"Because I love you, and because you love me, you stubborn little vixen." He moved and she heard something skitter across the hardwood floor. "I could throttle you for making me do this. Do you think I like slapping your ass with this thing? Do you think I want to hurt you?"

"You're not hurting me. I like it. Do it again."

"Katie?"

"Chris. I love the sting. Oh my God. I've never felt anything so erotic in all my life. Please?"

Movement again on the bed. One side gave way and it felt like he was reaching for something on the floor. Then, the slap on her ass again and she moaned in relief. "I could get used to this."

"You will marry me."

"I don't know..."

Again.

"I said, you *will* marry me."

Excitement thrilled up inside of her. "I may need more convincing."

"I'm going to turn you over my knee and let the palm of my hand do that convincing."

"Oh, yes. Do that. And I will marry you."

This time she knew he'd thrown the paddle because she was sure it bounced off the wall beside them.

He uncuffed her other hand then and pulled at her hips until her ass was up in the air. He ran his palms over the smooth skin of her cheeks and massaged. Katie moaned. The deliberately, one after the other, he delivered three firm swats to each cheek.

Beneath his hands, Katie quivered and gasped, her entire body shaking.

"I am so turned on," she whispered.

As was he. Turned on and throbbing hard. He twisted and grasped her buttocks, penetrating her with rigid, hot length of him from behind.

Groaning, he pumped in and out behind her while she clenched the blankets in her fists and held on, pressure building inside her just as tangible as the ring she knew was on her finger.

"Oh my God, Katie..." he groaned.

The notion that she pleased him sent trills over her spine as his hands snaked up her back and reached around to grasp her breasts. He pinched her nipples and that one act sent her over the edge with a shout, her body bucking and exploding with the release of pent-up passion and emotion. She rolled with it until it overcame her and then brought her back down to earth.

Gripping the sheets, she let him ride out the ride, and very soon, he shouted and trembled, tumbling over her and holding her close.

A few blissful minutes later, Chris untied the blindfold. He rolled back over her while kissing her face and threading his fingers through her hair.

"God, I love you," he moaned.

"I love you, too, Chris Marks."

"Marry me."

"Oh, yes. On one condition."

He arched a brow. "And that is?"

"Never stop spanking me."

"If that is the way to your heart, Katie Marie, then I'm happy to oblige."

"Oh yes. Never stop, Chris."

Grinning, he sat back and grasped her hips, pulling her closer. "Let's make another baby."

"I don't think it's possible to make another one while I'm already pregnant."

"Oh, yeah..."

But that didn't stop them from trying.

THE NEXT MORNING, Katie fingered the gorgeous platinum diamond ring on her left finger. Staring at the thing, she realized she had no clue having it there would make her so happy.

Exhaling long, she glanced at Chris sleeping beside her. He was exhausted. They had played all night, as was evident by their surroundings.

A dirty movie loop still played on the TV. The cheese-board was half-cocked on the nightstand with cheese cubes on the floor. Chris had downed the wine because she didn't want to drink. The bed restraints and cuffs hung over the side of the bed with other props and toys littered about the floor.

Smiling, she reached over and tugged the wave of hair falling over his forehead. "Wake up, sleepyhead," she whispered.

Without opening his eyes, he dragged her under the covers and pulled her into a bear hug. "There was something I forgot to ask you last night," he mumbled into his pillow.

"What's that?"

"Suzie will kill me."

"Suzie? Why?"

He was silent for another moment and then maneuvered so they were face to face on the pillow. "Dreams." He touched her lower lip with his fingertip, his eyes following the movement.

"Oh?"

Nodding, he continued. "What are your dreams, Katie Long?"

She studied his face and for the first time in her life, really and truly knew that her dream had come true. She'd just been too stubborn to know what her dream was.

"Somehow, what I thought was a dream, seems rather insignificant at the moment. I have everything I need right here."

He shook his head. "Dreams are important. And whatever yours is, I want you to have it."

"I have you." Nuzzling closer, she kissed him.

"And I have you. But whatever you want in your life,

Katie, whatever your dream, I want to know what it is, and I want you to pursue it. If I can help make that happen for you, I will do everything I can. And through it all, know that I'm not going anywhere. I'm right beside you, cheering you on."

"Okay. I will tell you." Tears stinging her eyes, she reached for his hand and laid it on her belly. "Later," she breathed. "I have you and I have our baby. That's all I need for now. My dreams will come when it's time."

"Yes." He leaned into to kiss her. "I love you, Katie Marie Long."

"I love you right back, Chris Marks."

Chapter Eight

"Well, there they go again." Sydney leaned over the doughnut case and stared out the bakery front window. "And the Labrador is heading straight for Bea across the street."

Suzie heard the tone of her cousin's voice and followed her gaze. "Hells bells. That girl. You stay with the shop, and I'll herd the animals."

She wiped her hands on a kitchen towel and whipped off her apron. Last thing they needed this morning was another episode with dogs and customers. With one eye on Lyssa Larkin and another on the dogs scattered on the sidewalk, Suzie was thankful for the fifteen-mile-an-hour speed limit on North Main. She spied Bea across the street, who was rushing to unlock the library door and get inside. She was afraid of dogs.

With Katie and Chris off on their honeymoon—a week in New York so Katie can meet with a potential publisher, and to explore the possibility of living in the Big Apple for a few weeks before the baby comes—Bea was manning the library by herself. Last thing the town needed was an incapacitated librarian assistant due to dog bite.

"Matt!" With a glance and a shout, she alerted her brother-in-law police officer. His morning coffee would have to wait. "Dog run amok at twelve o'clock!" She pushed through the bakery crowd. "I need backup," she told him. "Bring friends."

She edged by a man entering the bakery who sidestepped her while checking his cell phone messages. "Oh, excuse me. Sorry," she said, bumping him from the side.

He looked up. "No worries. All okay?"

Suzie shook her head. "Just morning puppy rescue," she returned.

His face held a puzzled look but Suzie didn't stick around long enough to explain. For the next several minutes she, Matt, and a couple of coffee-goers helped herd Lyssa Larkin's puppy mess while Lyssa stood on the sidewalk frantically calling out dog names and grabbing leashes.

"Oh God, the Labrador is taking a whiz on the newspaper stand!"

Dammit. It wasn't the first time this had happened. Lyssa's new puppy nanny business was experiencing a ton of growing pains.

"Take the Shih Tzu!" She handed the leash to Lyssa.

"Thank you! Oh God, Suzie, I'm so sorry!"

Suddenly it seemed half of Harbor Falls' residents were scrambling in an attempt to capture all of the dogs. Finally, Suzie, out of breath and breaking a sweat, caught up with Lyssa who was now holding tightly onto several leashes with critters in tow.

"Do a head count?"

"Seven." Lyssa huffed out a breath. "There are seven. That's right. Moose, Gilda, Jeremiah, Sophie, Crackers, Spot, and Harold."

"Harold?"

"He's the Standard Poodle."

Suzie shook her head and noticed the crowd around them

dissipating. "Lyssa, you either need to chain those dogs to your body or get another profession."

"But I love the dogs!"

"Then control them! I can't do this every morning."

Lyssa eyed her. "It's not every morning, Suzie. Seriously." She rolled her eyes. "Besides, it wasn't my fault. Mrs. Pierson's cat, Mellow Yellow, jumped out of the alley and scared Crackers—he's the Chihuahua—and started him barking. Then Sophie, who doesn't really like little dogs at all, got annoyed at Crackers and started lunging at the little guy. Then, Jeremiah, the Lab, spotted Bea across the street and well... Well, it was all over then."

Suzie shook her head and glanced toward the bakery. "It's not good for business, Lyssa, all of this commotion. People will stop coming. You understand that, right?"

Lyssa bit her lip. Suzie knew the woman was trying to make a living and she appreciated that, but Lyssa really needed to get a grip on things. Literally.

The bakery door opened and the man Suzie nudged earlier exited. He paused for a moment, looking down at his cell phone again and scrolling with one hand. In the other, he balanced a cup of coffee and a bag of pastries.

Lyssa shouted. "Harold no!"

Harold, at that moment, mistook the gentleman's leg for a fire hydrant, and sprinkled on his shoe.

"No, no, no, no!" Lyssa jerked all of the dogs, and they started barking in unison.

Suzie shouted to the man over the cacophony. "Oh my God. So sorry!" Then back to Lyssa, she ordered, "Get the dogs out of here! I'll handle this."

Lyssa's face twisted into a grimace and then she mouthed the words, *I'm sorry*, and took off with the dogs, tripping and skipping down the street trying to keep up with them. Suzie turned back to the man.

"I am so sorry. Let me get some towels inside. The bakery will pay for cleaning everything."

He stared at his shoe and the damp cuff of his trousers, and then lifted his gaze to stare at Suzie. "No worries," he said. "I have puppies."

"Then you understand."

"Sort of. I'm learning."

"Oh great. We'll still pay. Please bring the cleaning bill by."

He nodded. "Sure."

Then he left. Quickly. Without a backward glance. Suzie didn't blame him.

Huffing out a quick breath, she glanced back down the street in the opposite direction, following Lyssa Larkin as she stumbled after and tried to control her collection of canines.

Lord a mercy. That woman.

A Note from Maddie

Friends,

That Katie Long. I thought she'd never commit to Chris. Did you enjoy their little story? I hope we see more of them in future books. What do you think?

If you enjoyed reading *Tame My Heart*, then please consider sharing with others. One of the best ways to tell others about the book is to leave a review at Goodreads, or at the bookstore where you purchased the book. You can also leave reviews at my website, maddiejamesbooks.com.

Ready for more Sweet Hart Inn? Scroll on to read the first chapter of *The Dating Game*. You got a glimpse of Lyssa Larkin, the puppy nanny, in this book. Scroll on to read chapter one!

The Dating Game

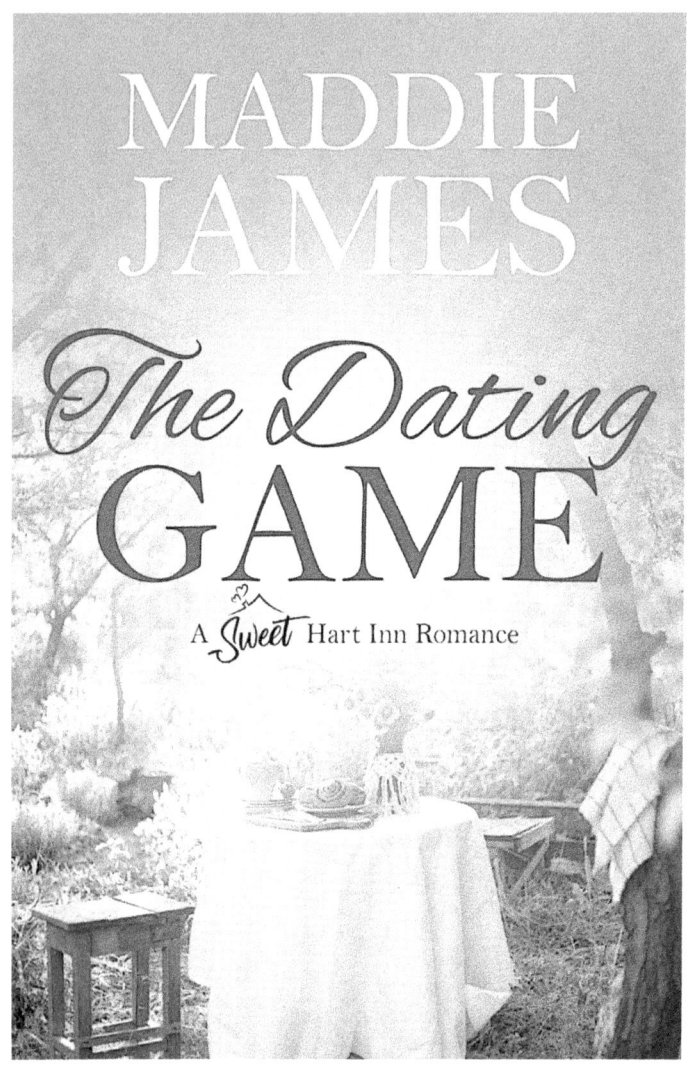

MADDIE JAMES

The Dating GAME

A Sweet Hart Inn Romance

Chapter One—The Dating Game

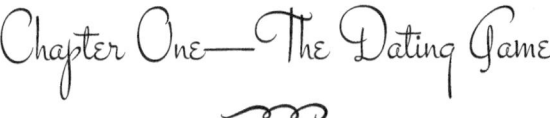

"I give up. To hell with men. I'll just stick with dogs from now on."

Sydney Hart watched Lyssa Larkin daub at the sugar rim gracing her upper lip and then dip a cinnamon-powdered doughnut into her heavily creamed coffee, and frowned. Lyssa dunk-dunk-dunked the thing, leaning over the coffee cup. Her long, brunette ponytail slid over her shoulder while she stuffed the rest of the doughnut into her mouth.

Sydney handed Lyssa a napkin. "Your chin," she said.

Lyssa nodded and swiped again.

"So, you're giving up on men." Sydney stated.

Lyssa rolled her big brown eyes. "I'm an old maid, Sydney. No one wants an old maid. Men expect a thirty-six-year-old woman has had *some* experience with men. Most men assume that you have already been married and divorced by my age. Had kids even. Me? I've only had sex with two men and have never been married, no kids, and no stinking divorce! Men just don't understand that. They wonder what is wrong with me. I'm an anomaly."

"There is nothing wrong with you, Lyssa. You're beautiful, smart, and a catch."

"I'm pudgy."

Sydney cleared her throat. "Well, you're working on that, right? I mean, with all of the dog-walking..." Sydney wasn't sure she wanted to go there.

Lyssa peered. "Yes. I guess I am. I've just been in a funk lately."

Sydney waved her off. "Like I said, you're beautiful just the way you are, Lyssa. My goodness, you were Homecoming Queen!"

"Tell that to the guys who look at you cross-eyed when you say you've never been married. Besides, Homecoming Queen was twenty years ago. No one remembers that."

Except you keep reminding us. "That's ridiculous. Women older than you marry for the first time all the time."

"Maybe in the big cities but Sydney, this is Harbor Falls. Population 6,232. Small, southern, Bible belt and all that. It's weird here."

"Hm."

"So now you get it?"

Leaning in, Sydney looked into Lyssa's eyes. "How old am I?"

Lyssa blinked. "Um, you're thirty-two, I think."

She nodded. "That's right. Do you see me going off the deep end because I don't have a man in my life right now?"

"But you date."

"Ha! Occasionally."

"But you're married to your business."

"And that gets damned old. Don't you think I don't want a man? I'm human, Lyssa, just like you but I don't go around moping about it all the time."

"Well, I'm four years older than you. Wait until you are thirty-six."

Rolling her eyes, Sydney said, "Let me get this straight." She braced herself against the counter, her palms flat on the Formica top. "You're forgetting men and throwing your life to the dogs."

"Why not?" Lyssa shrugged and reached for another sugared treat. "Dogs love me. Mostly. I mean, I'm still learning but I get along with dogs. And they can be so cuddly and warm, and their love—" Lyssa lifted another sweet treat toward her mouth "—their love is unconditional. I've never had unconditional love from any man."

Sydney put her palm over Lyssa's hand. "Lyssa. That's three. Don't you think...?"

Lyssa's baby browns narrowed and she glared daggers. Sydney jerked her hand back.

"Listen to what I am saying, Sydney," Lyssa bit out, "I don't have sex. I don't drink. I don't smoke pot or do drugs. I don't even drink diet soda much, although some might say that I should. So let me have the damned doughnut, you hear me?"

Sydney nodded. She would give her that. *Poor thing.*

"Today I need the damn doughnut," Lyssa muttered, staring in her mug.

Sydney exhaled and glanced away from the sugarcoated disaster and toward the bakery entrance. The bell over the door tinkled. Sighing, she moved around the counter and rushed to take a box from the woman struggling with the door.

"Give me that."

Suzie Hart Matthews stepped inside the bakery and blew out a breath. "Thank you!" A breeze whipped in behind them and slapped the door flat open against the wall. "Oh!"

Sydney angled the box on the counter and raced to catch the door before the wind slammed it back again and broke the old glass windowpane insets.

"A bit brisk," Suzie said, straightening her jacket about her.

Sydney firmly shut the door. "You can say that again. It's April, for sure. Thunderstorm coming, I think." Turning, she glanced toward her cousin, Suzie, and then at Lyssa, who was daubing off another round of powdered sugar on her Dusty Pink-lined lips and staring into her empty cup.

Lyssa glanced up. "Mind if I refill my coffee, Syd?"

"Have at it."

Both Sydney and Suzie watched as Lyssa slid off the counter bar stool and waddled in her black stretch pants around the counter and toward the Bunn coffeemaker. Suzie sidled closer to Sydney and whispered. "Put on a tad bit of weight lately, huh?"

In a low voice, Sydney replied, "She's depressed. Is throwing her life to the dogs."

Suzie slanted a gaze her way. "You don't say."

"Yeah. Well, she's sworn off men and is devoting herself to a life of puppy nannyism. Or so she says. I think she's also worshipping at the sugar altar."

One corner of Suzie's mouth drew up. "You're right. She's definitely depressed. That girl will eat her way into the next size up in no time."

Lyssa shouted out from across the room. "I took the last of it, Syd. Should I make a new pot?"

"Sure thing, hon. Go for it."

They watched her twiddle with the carafe and the filter and the basket, punching buttons and listening for the first drips to hiss against the bottom of the stainless-steel carafe.

"So, what do you think?" Sydney prodded.

"What do you mean?"

"Can you fix her up with someone? I mean, your luck is pretty much spot-on lately. Can you take on Lyssa?"

"No." Suzie turned to face Sydney. "I'm not getting

caught up in this. I'm exhausted after that last bout with Chris and Katie."

"But that worked out fine. Heck, they are on their honeymoon already. Right? And Mary and Nash are into their married lives. Not to mention how you got Shelley and Matt back together. You're good, Suzie. You can do this for Lyssa."

"I know. But she's, well...."

"I get it. But maybe you can turn things around for her."

Suzie shook her head. "I dunno. This will require..." She glanced again at Lyssa, who was waiting for the carafe to fill while inspecting her teeth in the wall mirror behind the counter. "Oh hell, face it Syd, Lyssa is just different."

"But she's a good person. Truly. Just a little high maintenance, is all."

Suzie snorted.

"C'mon, Suze. You were never one to hold back on a challenge. Besides, I'll help you. Promise."

"What I really need is to get started on preparations for that party tonight."

"So, say you'll give it a thought and then we'll get busy."

Crossing her arms over her chest, Suzie forced a thin breath through her lips. "All right. I can find her a man, but she has to stop eating. Those stretch pants are going pop if she looks at another doughnut."

Sydney snickered. "I'll get her off the sugar. You get her a man. Deal?"

Suzie gave her a crooked grin. "Deal."

"What's in the box, Suzie?"

Both women turned to find Lyssa headed their way again, cradling a mug of coffee in both hands. She sniffed the brew in her cup, settled back on her stool, glanced to the edge of the counter and with a forefinger, attempted to lift the lid on the large pastry box.

Sydney placed a gentle finger on the lid, preventing it from opening.

Lyssa shot her a glance.

Suzie said, "Key lime tarts, blueberry scones, and my famous Cinna-Mocha Brownie Fudge Cupcakes."

Lyssa's smile widened and her eyebrows popped wider. "Oh?" She stood and leaned toward the box.

This time, Suzie laid a firm hand on the lid. "They are for a party we're catering this evening, Lyssa." Then turning to Sydney, she said, "Did Shelley get to Asheville to get that dipping chocolate? I can't make my dipped fruit without it."

Nodding, Sydney reached for the box. "Yes. She called and is on her way. I'd say she'll be here about three. In the meantime..." She stopped. "Lyssa? What are you doing tonight? We could use another hand at the Talbert reception later. It's at the Lodge."

Lyssa stared at her. "You mean. Work? Me?"

Suzie closed her eyes.

Sydney shook her head.

"Excuse me, Lyssa." Sydney's sarcasm was thick. "We totally forgot that ex-Homecoming Queens with trust funds do not work. How dare us?"

Lyssa stood, obviously flustered. "I do too work! I have a job, and you know it! I am the best damned puppy nanny in Harbor Falls!"

"You're the only puppy nanny in Harbor Falls," Suzie quipped. "And of course we know you work. We see you walking—and losing—those dogs every morning. I just thought maybe you'd like to pick up some extra cash, and we could talk about your, um, man problem."

"Man problem?" Lyssa's voice rose an octave. "Sydney, you *told her*?"

"Well, I..."

All at once, Lyssa plopped back on her stool and the tears spilled. "Damn you. Damn both of you. Will you never let me forget that queen thing? The old maid thing? The trust fund thing? Can I help it if my grandmother left me with a house and a little extra cash? And while we're at it, can we also put a halt on the Lyssa-is-too-fat-and-will-never-find-a-man thing?"

"That last one is all in your head, Lyssa Larkin, and you know it." Sydney crossed her arms over her chest and looked down at her.

Lyssa snorted a sob and powdered sugar flew.

"Oh hell." Suzie parked her fists on her hips. "Lyssa Larkin, what the peach cobbler is wrong with you? You are making no sense. All we wondered is if you wanted to make a little cash. Your choice. Thought maybe you'd quit moping around and get out and have some social interaction. I'd forgotten about the Homecoming thing years ago, even if you did beat me out and you were only a sophomore. Still, all you ever had to do was bat those big brown eyes of yours and every teacher in the school and every boy on the football team came running to do your bidding. So, what's the deal here, huh? Get out of this funk, forget the past, and if you know what's good for you, quit eating those damned doughnuts!"

All that said really didn't make a difference because Lyssa took one more long look between the cousins and burst into tears again. This time, full throttle.

"Shit." Sydney's hands fluttered into the air, and she headed toward the back and the kitchen. She had too much work to do prepping for tonight to stand there and listen to Lyssa's grumbling. But Suzie stayed behind, and Sydney overheard her talking some nonsense to Lyssa. Something about drying her tears and meeting her at the inn tomorrow to figure things out.

Lyssa whined something about having to pick up a dog in

the morning from a client. Their voices faded and Sydney heard the familiar tinkle of the bell over the door.

"Thank God," she muttered. "Get her out of my bakery before she eats me out of house and business!"

Continue the series with *The Dating Game!*

The Dating Game

THE *Dating* GAME

HARBOR FALLS ROMANCE: SWEET HART INN
MADDIE JAMES

More Sweet Hart Inn

Cozy up at the inn where the heart of the Blue Ridge beats strongest...

WELCOME TO SWEET HART INN, a charming bed and breakfast nestled along the peaceful shores of Falls Lake, at the foot of Falls Mountain. At the center of it all is chef and innkeeper Suzie Hart, whose kitchen is always warm, and whose heart is always open. Together with her husband Brad, Suzie serves up matchmaking advice and comfort food, along with second chances, and a generous helping of happily ever after.

The Sweet Hart Inn Books

All of My Heart
Take My Heart
Match My Heart
Tame My Heart
The Dating Game
Miss Matched Hearts
The Husband List
Chase My Heart
No Sweeter Match
One More Kiss

The Falls Mountain Books

Welcome to Falls Mountain, and the quaint town of Harbor Falls.

Tucked deep into the Blue Ridge Mountains, bricked streets, lakeside views, and charming local shops set the scene for small town romance.

In this standalone-but-interconnected series, you'll meet bakers, bookstore owners, chocolatiers, school teachers, and more—all trying to run their businesses, chase their dreams, and keep their hearts in check. But in Harbor Falls, love has a habit of showing up unannounced...

From second chances to secret babies to grumpy-sunshine pairings, each book brings a satisfying happily-ever-after and a cast of characters you'll want to visit again and again.

Falls Mountain Romance is a companion series to the Sweet Hart Inn Romance books by Maddie James.

Dance into My Heart
The Christmas Nanny
The Heartbreaker

Star Crossed
Not This Christmas
Convince My Heart

I hope you'll check out these books, and my other series, on my website at:
www.maddiejamesbooks.com

About Maddie James

Romance with a pulse—small towns, big love, and a dash of drama.

Maddie James writes small-town romance with heart, heat, and the occasional haunting. Her stories range from sweet to spicy, suspenseful to supernatural—happily-ever-afters guaranteed! From stand-alone love stories to binge-worthy series, Maddie delivers love next door, some cowboy kisses, an occasional hint of danger, and just enough drama to keep things interesting.

Get all the drama delivered to your inbox when you sign-on to Maddie's VIP reader list!
Free books, sneak peaks, bonus content, giveaways, and more...
Learn more: maddiejamesbooks.com/pages/newsletter

www.ingramcontent.com/pod-product-compliance
Lightning Source LLC
Chambersburg PA
CBHW072032170626
46811CB00008B/3039